THE ACCIDENTAL BENEFACTOR

Anne David

Dear Mary,
Enjoy the story!
Anne David

THE ACCIDENTAL BENEFACTOR

First edition. March 18, 2016.

Copyright © 2016 Anne David.

Written by Anne David.

To all of the gold bugs in the world.

September 2013

Chapter 1

Kansas City

The warm summer breeze ruffled the sheer curtains of the bedroom window and brushed the leaves on the great oak tree just outside. Birds had been singing, but stopped when the gun went off. Inside the bedroom, in a direct line from the window to the open hall door, lay the crumpled body of a small gray haired man.

Standing in the hallway in front of the bedroom door was a dazed gray haired woman. She was staring at the gun in her hand and thought she saw smoke coming out of the barrel. She hadn't realized that guns really smoked when they were fired. She had never held a gun before and wondered why she had picked this one up. She could see that it had been a mistake. What was she going to do?

She edged closer to the body on the floor holding the gun at arm's length. He certainly looked dead, even though she couldn't see any blood. But then she couldn't detect any movement of his chest either. She watched him for a few minutes to be sure and then slowly backed out of the room, gun still in her hand. She hurried down the front hall staircase to the telephone table where she gently laid down the gun and picked up the phone. She hoped that Adele would know what to do.

Addie Whitaker was on the phone with a vendor when Aunt Helen rang in. She didn't answer. She would just have to call her back as she was in hard negotiations over the purchase of a display case for the dangle earrings she was thinking of adding to their inventory.

"Michael, why don't we do this," Addie said, in what she hoped was a persuasive tone. "Why don't we just use the display case on a trial basis and see how the earrings sell. Then if they are a hit, I'll buy the case."

"That's fine," agreed Michael Kahn. They both knew that Addie's little store survived on a very slim margin. He was glad to let her use the case. It got his merchandise into her store, *and* it got him into the store. "I'll bring it by when your order comes in."

"Great! When do you think that'll be?" She hoped to be out then so that she wouldn't have to face him about the overdue invoice on the jeweled evening bags she bought three months ago. She felt bad about it. She liked him and thought he might like her. So it was certainly no way to treat a friend. But then, what are friends for if not to bail you out occasionally. And she needed all the bailing out she could get.

It had been over a year since she had come back to Kansas City, something she had not planned to do. She had left for greener pastures when her mother had died five years ago leaving behind her only remaining relatives, her mother's two older sisters, Aunt Rose, the entrepreneur who managed a small shop, and Aunt Helen, the homemaker. But her aunts were getting older and she was all the family they had. And, while they hadn't come out and directly asked her to come back, there was an unstated hope that was hard to ignore. What they said was, "if you could just give us some advice about the store," but what they really meant was "HELP!"

For years her two spinster aunts had made a living from selling used quality furniture at their small second hand furniture store, The Vintage House, which Addie thought sounded like a wine bar, and would probably have been more profitable, supplemented by the small amount of money they got from renting out a room in their very large, but gently aging home. The store was Aunt Rose's domain and, in the past, they had been able to live off of the small profit it produced. She had been the first to bid at estate sales, where she got most of their merchandise, and quick to take on consignment pieces, so her good taste in inventory brought in their clientele. But she was losing the technology battle. Now the younger dealers were beating her to the punch. They bought and sold with their computers and she was left with a dwindling choice of inventory.

Addie had taken stock of the situation and decided that they needed to update their image and become more relevant to a younger generation of homeowners than her aunts had been serving. She had gradually added new inventory that complimented the furniture. High-end decorative accessories and jewelry began to fill shelving that had been left unused. Armoires that were for sale opened up their doors and displayed elegant antique linens and sachets meant to bring France to the Midwest. Of course, these additions to the inventory meant additions to expenses. And so, Addie found that she had joined the ranks of the many small businesses that juggled their profits at the end of the month, deciding who should be paid first. It was a constant struggle to keep the wolf from the door. And there was more than one wolf.

Once the word got out that there was an attractive young woman running the shop, vendor reps began showing up. Michael was one of the nicer ones. At least he wasn't so obvious about his intentions, which is why she found herself saying yes to the evening bags and the jewelry that he represented. Although, it was beginning to nag at her that he let her shift his invoices to the back of the line without the usual browbeating that came from other companies – OVERDUE was a word that was beginning to take over her dreams.

"I can't say how long it will take," Michael answered. "I'll just drop by with it when it comes in." He knew if he gave her an actual date and time she would probably be out. He didn't know if she was trying to avoid him or his invoices. He would give it a little more time. There was a click on the line. "Is that your phone?" he asked.

"Oh, god, I forgot. It's my aunt. She called in a few minutes ago. I need to answer. I'll see you when you bring the case." She paused a second. "And Michael, thanks."

"You bet." That sounded promising.

Addie clicked over to the other line. "Helen, I'm sorry I didn't get right back to you. What's up?"

"Adele, I think you'd better come home." Helen's voice sounded small to Addie.

"We're closing the store in another hour, so we should be home by 6:30."

"Dear, I don't think this should wait that long," she sounded as if she might cry.

"What is it?" Addie was starting to worry. This aunt was a true flibbertigibbet, for want of a better word, but she rarely cried.

"It's Mr. Barker. I think he's dead."

"Good heavens Helen! What do you mean?" Mr. Barker was their renter.

"I mean he isn't breathing. At least it doesn't look like it." Her voice trailed off.

"You need to call 911!"

"Oh, I just can't do that!" Helen's voice was rising in pitch.

"Calm down," Addie used her soothing voice. "Why can't you call?"

"I don't know how I would ever explain it!"

"You won't have to explain anything. Just tell them to send an ambulance. Are you sure he's dead? You probably should have called for help before now. How do you know he's dead?"

"Well, I went in and looked at him. He's right there on the floor. I watched his chest and it didn't move," she hesitated. "I didn't see any blood," she finished.

"Blood! Why would you see blood?"

"Well, I just assumed when someone was shot there would be blood."

"Shot? Shot!" now Addie felt a sense of panic taking over. "How do you know he was shot?"

"Oh dear. This why I didn't want to call 911." There was a short pause. *"I shot him!"*

Addie didn't ask any more questions, just told Helen to sit down and wait until she got there.

"Rose!" she called out to her other aunt who was in the stockroom counting napkins or something. "We have to close up now." She was already shutting down the cash register and turning the sign in the door to Closed. Unfortunately, she didn't have to shoo any customers out of the shop.

"Oh my, is it six already?" said Rose, coming from the back of the store. She peered at the clock on the counter. "Oh no dear, it's only five. It's a little early to close."

"Well, today we need to close early." Addie already had her purse and car keys in her hand. "There's a little problem at home."

"Oh lands! There's nothing wrong with Helen is there?" They each worried about the other's health. Helen had once told Addie that they hoped they would leave this world at the same time because neither wished to be left by themselves.

"No, Helen is ok. It's Mr. Barker."

"Oh dear. He's not leaving us is he?"

"I think he might be," said Addie and put the car into gear.

Mr. Barker had rented a room in their house for the past twenty plus years and they had come to consider him part of the family. They also counted on the little income it brought in. Mr. Barker came to town only once a month, and then only stayed for the weekend. Once a year he would stay for a week, which he said was his vacation week, but he insisted on paying them as if he was there all of the time. He said that the room, and their house, was like a home to him, and while he couldn't be there all of the time, it gave him comfort to think about it while he was on the road. It was an odd arrangement, to be sure, but one that had settled into a routine years ago.

"Oh, I just can't imagine him not being there," Rose worried. Addie had recently found herself fixating on Aunt Rose's habit of starting almost every sentence with "Oh." She would have to get over it or say something to Rose because it was becoming annoying. Addie was letting her mind wander in any direction it wanted to as she raced to get home. It was too bizarre to think about what was waiting for them there.

Addie turned the car into the driveway and pulled up under the portico by the side door of the stately old home. It had been a beauty in its day, but that was long ago. This neighborhood had been the cultural center of the city in the early part of the last century, but it had fallen on hard times and had gradually wasted away. Many of the large homes had been divided up, too big to heat and cool, and multiple families filled them now bringing with them all of their vehicles. Pick-up trucks and cars crowded the curbs at all hours. Addie wondered when people went to work. But the street was wide and still shaded by grand old oak trees and on a warm summer day like this the ragged edges of life were blurred.

Addie was out of the car and up the steps before Rose had gotten out.

"Adele, why are you in such a hurry?" Rose called as she trailed behind her through the door and into the cool dimness of the central hall.

"Helen?" Addie called out.

"In here," came the answer from the parlor.

Aunt Helen was sitting on the edge of the Victorian sofa that was the central focus of the room. She was nervously twisting a handkerchief in her lap and her eyes looked teary.

"Oh, I'm so glad you've come! I'm just beside myself with worry. Whatever will become of me?" and she finally let the tears flow. Addie found herself thinking that Helen did it too, the 'Oh' thing.

"Helen!" Rose had been alarmed when they had made such a hurried trip home, but now she was horrified to see her sister in such a state. "What's wrong?"

"Everything is wrong!" said Helen between sobs. "Mr. Barker is dead and I'm going to jail!" She punctuated that dramatic statement with a very unladylike blow of the nose into her handkerchief.

Rose sat down on a side chair. She was sure that she hadn't heard that right. As if she read her mind, Helen said it again.

"Mr. Barker is dead and I killed him. I'm sure they will send me to jail. I've been sitting here thinking about it and I don't see how it could turn out any differently."

Rose turned to Addie. "What on earth is she talking about?"

Addie shook her head. "This is all I know myself." She turned to Helen. "Let's start from the beginning. What happened?"

Helen looked at each of them and said in a very beseeching voice, "It was an accident. You just have to believe me."

"Of course, we believe you, but we need to hear the story."

"Alright," Helen closed her eyes for minute then sat up straight and recounted the horrendous event.

"I went upstairs this afternoon to see if Mr. Barker would like to have supper with us this evening. He always seems so lonely and I just thought that since this was his vacation week he might like to have a home cooked meal. I know he likes to be by himself when he's just here on weekends, but I think it would be good for him to have a little slice of family life once in a while."

"Helen! Try to stay with the story about the shooting." Addie was beginning to feel the way Rose looked right now. Bewildered was the best description. Aunt Helen could be bewildering in the best of circumstances.

"Yes, well when I came up the stairs I could see that his bedroom door was open and I could see something laying on the floor in front of his door."

"Mr. Barker?" Rose's voice had taken on a strange shrill timbre.

"No, not Mr. Barker. Something small. So I went along to where it was and it was a gun. I picked it up, and oh how I wish I had never done that, but I did." She paused.

"Then what!" Addie knew she must have said that too loud based on the startled looks from her aunts.

"It went off."

They were all quiet. Addie had heard about silence being deafening, but it wasn't. She could plainly hear her pulse beating and thought the others must hear it too.

Helen went on. "Well, the noise was so loud and I was so startled that I just stood there. When I looked in Mr. Barker's room he was lying on the floor. I had shot him, you see."

"You said that you didn't see any blood," Addie reminded her.

"No, I didn't and that surprised me. I always thought shootings were supposed to be so messy. But I didn't look underneath him. Maybe all of the blood is under him."

Rose finally stirred on her chair. This was what she had always feared. Helen was going gaga on her. It always seemed that one or the other of them dying first would be the worst thing to happen, but now she knew it wasn't. Living with the other one and their delusions would be worse. Probably Alzheimer's...early stages.

Addie took a deep breath and then said, "We need to go see Mr. Barker."

"Oh yes, I know we must," Helen agreed reluctantly. "I knew we'd have to look at him again. I just couldn't do it by myself though."

"We'll all go up together and it won't seem so bad," Addie reassure her aunt even though she wasn't reassuring herself. "What did you do with the gun, by the way?"

"It's right here, dear. I left it on the hall table."

They followed her into the hall and observed the gun right where she said it would be, on the table next to the phone. It was small and black. They all stared at it.

"It looks like a toy," Rose said finally. "But where would a toy come from? There aren't any children here."

"It's not a toy, I can assure you!" Helen sounded almost indignant and her voice rose in pitch. In fact they were all talking in a much higher pitch than usual.

"Now Aunties. Let's just go see about Mr. Barker. We'll worry about the gun later. Don't touch it!" Rose looked as if she might be thinking of picking it up.

"That's right," said Helen. "It's sure to be evidence."

"Well, that's the point then!" declared Rose. "We should wipe it clean in case you've left fingerprints on it!"

It was amazing how fast Rose had gone from disbelief to complicity.

"Come on," urged Addie. "We need to go upstairs." She started up the staircase followed closely by the two older women.

Light streamed through the open door to Mr. Barker's room into the hallway. It was a corner room facing north and west and the sun wouldn't set for several more hours. The evening sun was brilliant. The three women walked cautiously toward the room and peered in. There he was. Mr. Barker, laid out on the floor and motionless.

"There! You see!" said Helen. "He's just where I left him."

"Of course he is! He's dead!" said Rose indignantly.

One would think that it was Rose who fired the shot thought Addie. "Stay where you are," she said. "Let me look at him." She needn't have worried that they would rush in the room ahead of her. They huddled closer to each other and watched as Addie went in to inspect Mr. Barker.

He was obviously dead and there was no blood in sight, so nothing new. Maybe Helen was right and there was blood underneath him. It meant Addie would have to move the body to find out. Before she did that maybe she could see a bullet hole, but there was nothing visible. He was wearing an open collared white dress shirt, his usual attire whenever she had seen him. He didn't seem to own casual clothes. His graying hair was thin, and always neatly groomed. When Addie thought about him, which she rarely did, pleasant was the word that came to mind. She realized that she knew very little about him even though he had rented this room for over twenty years.

"Oh Adele, come away," pleaded Helen.

"I'm just going to see if I can look underneath him," answered Addie struggling with a rising feeling of apprehension. Kneeling down next to the body she took a hold on the shoulder seam of his shirt and pulled up. His body lifted just enough so that she could see part way under him. No blood that she could see. She let go and he settled back onto the floor.

"I don't see anything," she reported. "I just can't imagine what happened Helen. If he's shot, then it was an amazing shot. I can't see a hole in him and I don't see any blood." She stood up and looked around the room. Everything seemed as usual, orderly. The room was large and the furnishings were comfortable; an old-fashioned four-poster bed, an easy chair with an ottoman, a side table, and a large oak dresser with a mirror. The windows were covered with old-fashioned lace curtains that were still gently stirring in the breeze, and they were completed with old-fashioned roller shades, rolled up at the moment, their crocheted pulls dangling at the end of their cords. Everything about the room was old-fashioned, even the dark oak wainscoting that skirted the walls. What Addie realized as she look around the room was there were almost no personal touches; no family pictures, no plants, no knick-knacks. There were several pictures on the wall, but they were generic scenes of early Kansas City. A newspaper, lying on the floor, was open to the crossword puzzle and his wood working case was sitting on the table, open. There was an old-fashioned lamp with a flowered globe and an alarm clock on the dresser next to a travel shaving kit. Nothing of the man, but then maybe it was the man.

"We need to call 911," Addie said. Her aunts nodded, but said nothing. They moved closer to each other. "We'll say we just found him. I don't think there's anything to worry about." She sounded calmer than she felt.

There was a phone in the upstairs hall and she called from there.

Chapter 2

A short heavyset man sat sweating in his car down the street from the old house. He periodically ran his handkerchief over his face and neck but it didn't help for long. He'd been sitting in the car for several hours and the late afternoon sun slanting through the windshield, combined with the closeness of the car, and his proclivity to sweat in any climate, had brought him to this soggy state. He wished he had a towel instead of a handkerchief.

Harry Crespi had watched George Cravetz for a long time. Not here in Kansas City, in Las Vegas where they both worked at the same establishment, one of the big casinos. Cravetz was in the bookkeeping department and Harry was part of the *accounting group*. He liked to say that it was his job to make the deadbeat gamblers account for themselves! Harry was pretty good at what he did and he made decent money. But he wanted more. He had developed a pretty good nose for cheats, being one himself, and his instincts told him George Cravetz was a cheat. He was too perfect. He did the same thing day in and day out, year in and year out. Only someone with a plan, or a screw loose, could go on like that. Harry was betting it was the first. He certainly had the right job to make himself a little extra money on the side and Harry was ready to take his share.

He wanted to get him alone and outside of Las Vegas so he followed him when he left on his yearly vacation. Imagine his surprise when George didn't take off for the desert like everyone supposed. He went to a hick burgh in the Midwest instead. Harry wondered if George was deviating from his usual routine, and, if he was, did it mean something – like he was getting ready to split with the money. Harry was positive now that there was money involved. He took the next flight to Kansas City after George left. He didn't want to be spotted. He and George weren't acquainted but they saw each other around the casino. He congratulated himself on locating Cravetz after the plane landed, although it hadn't been hard. He just checked with rental car agencies until he found the one that remembered George. The jerk thought he was slick using another name, but he was easy to describe.

He'd found Cravetz in his hidey-hole two days ago and had watched from down the block until he figured out the movements of the household. There were three women living there, two old ones and a young chick. One of the old broads and the young one left both mornings at 9:30 and came back at 6:30. He had followed them to a furniture store in a small shopping area. The young one unlocked the door so he figured the store belonged to them. He went back to the house and kept watching. The other old woman must be the housekeeper. He could see her go in and out with garbage and newspapers, sweep the steps and sidewalk, and hang out wet towels. She went out both days around four with an empty cloth shopping bag and came back close to five with groceries.

Cravetz was predictable, too. Both days he left the house at noon and drove to a small chain restaurant about a mile away for lunch. He returned there each day at six for dinner. He didn't blame the guy for wanting to eat by himself. Three women didn't make for great dinner companions. Now one woman, that was different. But not the old woman! He chuckled at himself.

This day had started out following the usual pattern. Nine thirty the two women left. At noon Cravetz left for lunch and was back by one. The old woman was in and out during the day doing house chores as usual. And she rewarded his vigilance by leaving the house at four with the shopping bag. Bingo! Now was his chance to make a move. He left his car parked down the street and walked with what he considered a confident stride, not too fast and not too slow, nothing that would draw attention to him. He went up the front porch steps and crossed the wide veranda to the door. Perfect. He knew he was hard to see here in the shadows. He reached out as if he were pressing the doorbell, but didn't. He didn't want to alert Cravetz to any kind of visitor. He tried the door and it was locked. No problem. He slipped a credit card from his wallet, jimmied it around the lock, and was inside in no time at all. He quietly closed the door behind him.

It felt pleasantly cool in the dimness of the hallway and he took a minute to let his eyes accommodate to the low light. He figured he had fifty minutes or so before the woman returned, but he wouldn't need that long, half an hour at the outside. He listened for a few minutes but the house was silent. He climbed the stairs to the second floor, the worn carpeting muffling his footsteps. He waited again but heard nothing. He could see a light coming under a door at the end of the hall. He walked toward it passing several open rooms on the way, their window shades pulled down against the summer sun. He hesitated in front of the door, sticking his right hand into his jacket pocket and wrapping his fingers around a small gun. He knocked with his left hand. He could hear feet shuffling inside.

"Yes?" came a reply and then the door opened to a room filled with the late afternoon sunlight.

"Hello George," said the small sweaty man.

"Who...? What are you doing here?" George was obviously unhappily surprised.

"Yeah, you know who I am, don't you. You were a little hard to find, but I managed." Harry pushed into the room and looked around. "So this is your Shangri-La? Seems like you'd want something a little more posh."

"What are you talking about?" George was becoming obviously agitated.

"See, I got sent out looking for ya'... because a large amount of money seems to be missing from the casino receipts." He didn't know if that was true but it would shake George up. "I was just thinking that you would be living a little higher on the hog, that's all. This sure ain't no hog. More like the sty." He was nosing around the room looking out the windows and poking at the travel kit on the dresser.

"What do you want?" asked George keeping his eyes on the hand in Harry's pocket.

"I'll get right to the point. I want a cut in the take."

George was quiet for a minute. "Then what? You'll go away? I should believe that?"

Harry was delighted. He was right about missing money. "Well, it don't matter if you believe it or not. I don't see that you got any choice. I could just knock you off and take it all, but I don't want that kind of trouble." At this point Harry had removed his hand from his pocket and was pointing the gun at George. "I just take a share, for not turning you in, see. Then I'll quietly disappear. No more trouble from me." He smiled at George.

"And when you don't return to the casino, then what?"

"Naw, it won't matter. I got plans to head to Mexico. Nobody's gonna look for me. Too much trouble with the drug business down there."

"I only have part of the money here," said George still tracking the gun. "I can give it to you and then I'll have to get the rest for you later."

"You must think I'm stupid. I'm sticking with you until we got the whole pile." He looked around the room. "How much do you have here?"

"I've got about $50,000 here and another $200,000 at a bank."

"At a bank? Well ain't you the business man." Harry looked at his watch. "It's four twenty. Banks don't close 'til six. We got time to go get the rest."

"Do you want the money that's here now?" George looked sick.

"Yeah, I want the money here. You said it. Let's start with that. Where is it?"

"It's in the case over there," and George nodded his head at the dresser.

"Great, get it out." Harry was back by the window looking toward the street. "Make it snappy though. That old broad will be coming back from the store soon."

George picked up the case and set it on the side table and began to unfasten the latches on the top. The case swung open towards him and was between him and Harry. "Here you go Harry. Let's start with this."

Harry turned towards him just as George raised an industrial nail gun out of the case and fired. It caught Harry between the eyes and he dropped to the floor with a reassuring thud. George was relieved to see that there was very little blood. But now what to do? He had to get the body out of here, but how? He knew Helen would be back soon and she could very well come knocking on his door. He grabbed Harry by his feet and began dragging him out into the hall toward the back steps. He knew he could get to the basement from here and park the body. He would work out some way to get rid of it tomorrow.

George thought about how hard he had worked all of these years to amass a small fortune, and it wasn't a measly $200,000. There was no way that he was going to let anyone stop him now, certainly not a cretin like Harry. He was sweating as he pulled the body behind him down the stairs. He would put him in one of those storage lockers in the back of the basement. Harry's head was bumping on the steps all of the way down to the first floor, but George didn't worry about the noise. The house was empty right now. He just needed to hurry. He flipped on the light at the top of the basement stairs and, looking down, realized that he would never be able to get the body back up. He would have to put him somewhere else. The garage. He dragged him through the kitchen to the service door to the side porch. When he stepped out he got a scare. There was a truck parked there in the driveway loaded with brush and small tree limbs, partially covered by a tarp. George stood very still just inside the door, listening. In the distance he could hear the crackle of brush being gathered up and then he remembered Helen telling him that someone was coming to clear the back yard. It was a big back yard with a lot of bushes and vines along the fence.

George looked at the truck again and the beginning of an idea took hold. The truck was parked close to the edge of the porch, which was almost as high as the side of the truck. Listening again, George decided the sounds were far enough away for what he had in mind. He grabbed Harry by the ankles and dragged him to the edge of the porch and then rolled him over the side into the truck. The body was sticking up on top of the brush so George pushed him down as far as he could against the inside of the truck and then pulled branches and leaves over him. He jerked the tarp over toward this side of the truck to cover the pile. There was room on the other side for whatever the gardener was still gathering. He stood up and looked at his work. He couldn't have planned it better, not that he had ever thought he would have to make a plan to get rid of a body.

He stepped back into the kitchen and went back to the service stairs. He held on to the railing for a moment. He felt queasy and cold. He wanted to get back upstairs to make sure there were no signs of Harry's visit. He congratulated himself on his quick thinking about the nail gun. His woodworking case contained a very compact but complete set of carpentry tools that he had used over the years to alter the storage capacity in his room, very cleverly he thought. No one could imagine the wealth stored behind the wainscoting that ran around the room or the value of the contents of the altered bed slat and the tall posts of the bedstead. But Harry said the casino sent him to bring him back.

They must have found out. He would have to get away from here, which meant packing up all of the gold. He wasn't ready to leave yet but he would have to. He'd have to make a plan, but first he needed to lie down. He was having trouble breathing.

George had gone to work more than forty years ago in the accounting department at the casino. And while he had a bookkeeper's demeanor, he was an entrepreneur at heart, but, alas, he also had a beer drinker's pocketbook. No money, just big dreams. He had been a diligent worker for many years and had gradually worked his way up to the head of the department. His employers liked him because he was loyal, discreet, deferential, and honest. How did they know he was honest? They checked him out. They knew that George led the life of a born loser, a type that they understood. He saved money from his modest salary and bought a small house in a cheap housing tract on the edge of Las Vegas; drove a small low priced Ford, which he traded in every five years, and got a good trade-in price because his mileage was always low; had a pension plan with the casino that required him to match their contribution, which, upon his retirement, would provide him with just slightly less money than he had been making; and he had a medical plan that offered nursing home care, since he had no family to take care of him in his old age. He spent his vacations camping in the desert, by himself, making sketches of the flora and fauna. And while he always invited fellow workers to join him, which was the yearly office joke, they always had other plans. Most importantly, the casino trusted George with the delivery of large amounts of money to their connections in Kansas City. The amounts hadn't been large at first, but as time went by, and the deliveries were impeccable, the cash entrusted to him had grown to impressive amounts. The casino bosses knew who George was.

George never tampered with these deliveries. He had a plan, his 'retirement plan' he called it, and it was vital to this plan that he could be trusted. The plan had evolved slowly at first, but then blossomed as George saw that it was possible to relieve the casino of a tidy sum of money over the years.

There were two critical events that put George onto his plan. First, he had read Harry Browne's *How You Can Profit From the Coming Devaluation.* The book turned George onto gold and he became a fervent believer. Second, when he was promoted to chief accountant, it became part of his duties to keep an accounting of a considerable amount of gold stored in a safe within the large casino vault. A private set of books was entrusted to George, nothing that was certified for the government. He never questioned the legality of his work or where the gold came from, for that matter, because it didn't take long for George to realize that the casino management paid little attention to it. It wasn't accessed often, only once or twice in as many years for good clients of the casino who preferred the anonymity of the metal. George wasn't sure why this account seemed neglected, but he appreciated the lack of interest on the part of the casino because he needed time to build his fortune.

He had started cautiously. At first he took a coin or two and adjusted the books. As time went on he took more coins, but never so many that he couldn't easily cover it in the accounting. And then one day he picked up a kilo bar off of the stack in the vault. It fit nicely into the palm of his hand. That's when a much more audacious plan began to form in his mind. He gently replaced the gold bar on the stack.

He realized that accounting tricks weren't going to work for this plan. It was one thing to take a few gold coins, but quite another to remove the gold bars. While no one paid much attention to the gold in the vault, they were sure to notice if the stacks dwindled and disappeared.

One evening, as he walked from the casino to his car, he stopped still in front of a shop that he had passed every day for some years. It was a shop that bought and sold gold and silver and offered a *fair price* for your jewelry. It caught his attention this evening because of a new window display. Bars of gold were stacked in a pyramid. George's first thought was that they were recklessly courting disaster. Anyone could smash the glass and take the gold. Then he realized that it surely couldn't be real gold. He knew now how he was going to make his new idea work.

In all of his bookwork at the casino he was scrupulously honest. And the big money that he delivered to Kansas City was another sign of his honesty and honesty was his cover, that and his mild mannered personality. He promoted himself as a Caspar Milquetoast double, with a large risk aversion mentality. As the years went on the illusion became a reality to the people he worked with. They never thought twice about George. He was steady. They laughed about him when he came back from his vacations and shared the pencil sketches he had done of the desert birds or cacti. He wanted them to laugh. If they were laughing, they believed the lie. Of course George never went to the desert. That's why he sketched the flora and fauna from birding books. You couldn't tell where he was with a sketch and you could with a photo. No, George spent his vacations in Kansas City.

He had realized early on that he needed to find a place to store his gold, somewhere else than in Las Vegas. Who knew if the management searched the houses of their employees, but stranger things had happened. When he first began making the casino's money deliveries, which were monthly, he had stayed in a two star hotel in downtown Kansas City. He would come in on a late Friday afternoon flight and return on Sunday afternoon. He realized then that he could transport his gold here when he made these trips for the casino, but where could he store it? He could keep it in a safety deposit box in a bank, but there were inherent problems with that. The government had made it illegal to own gold once and confiscated it. They could do it again. He wasn't a fan of the government and he wasn't going to lose his gold. A hotel obviously wouldn't do. He needed a small place of his own to come to each month. He didn't want to own a house because he would have to keep it up. A room would work. He found an ideal spot, a room in an old house in a gently declining part of the city. The two women who owned the house needed the extra income and were glad for a renter that was there only once a month. He insisted on paying them as if he was there full time, saying that it made him feel secure when he was traveling on the road so much to know that he had a place to come home to that was his.

The arrangement was perfect. The ladies respected his privacy and were delighted when he said he wanted to spruce up the room with his own money. Over the years he gradually added very handsome oak wainscoting around the room, which he stained a lovely walnut color. He bought himself a comfortable leather easy chair to add to the furnishings already there, a solid four-poster bed, an oak dresser, and a small side table. Because it was a corner room there were windows on two walls with peaceful views through large trees toward the street and the backyard. It was a comfortable gentleman's room.

He took his meals out. He said that he was a creature of habit and liked it that way and wouldn't want to be any bother to them. He was certainly no bother. They only had to launder linens once a month except the week that he came for his yearly vacation when he spent most of his time in the room working on his carpentry project. He was very tidy about it, too. He just installed one panel at a time making sure to clean up as he went.

He kept his tools in a case that he stored in the closet when he wasn't there.

In the early years the women had tried to engage him in conversations, but they were always short lived. He never seemed to have much to talk about. He never mentioned any family and his job sounded painfully dull. He said he sold plumbing fixtures to small contractors throughout the Midwest and northern states. The only personal information he had to offer was his name, Samuel Barker. But he was always pleasant and very polite. And, more importantly, he paid his rent on time.

George climbed slowly to the second floor leaning heavily on the hand railing. He stopped to catch his breath and tried to focus his eyes. There was a hazy aura around everything that he saw. As he walked toward his room he could see something lying in the hall in front of his door. He stopped and stared down at it and realized that it was the gun Harry had been holding. He should pick it up but his head was reeling and he was afraid he would collapse. He shuffled into his room and sank to the floor. He didn't know how long he lay there. He just knew that he could hardly draw a breath and everything had gone black. The last earthly sound George heard was the loud report of a gun. Then nothing.

Chapter 3

The siren sounds died down as the fire department paramedic vehicle pulled up in front of their house. Addie, Helen, and Rose had come back downstairs after making the 911 call. They had agreed that Addie should do the talking, but as of right now she had no idea what she would say. Should she tell them Helen's story? The paramedics were already rushing up the front porch steps as Helen opened the door. Out of the corner of her eye Addie saw Rose take a scarf from the coat rack and drop in on top of the gun.

"Where are we going ladies?"

"Upstairs," said Addie and she followed them as they hurried up the staircase. So far so good, no explanations asked for yet.

"The room at the end of the hall." But they were already there and they were vigorously applying CPR. They worked on Mr. Barker's body for what seemed to Addie like forever, but she could see that it wasn't doing any good.

"Sorry, Ma'am, he's not responding," said the medic. "We'll take him to the hospital, but I don't think you should get your hopes up."

They began moving his body onto the gurney that they had brought up with them and Addie held her breath. The specter of blood was still foremost in her thoughts. Nothing. The aging Persian carpet under Mr. Barker's body showed no signs of anything except the wear of many years.

Addie followed the men and the body down the stairs. She could see Helen and Rose huddled by the telephone desk, apparently trying to block it from view.

"I'll need some information ladies," said one of the young men. "Do you have a hospital preference?"

"Uh, no," Addie hesitated and then added, "the closest one would be best."

"We need the man's name and the hospital will want his insurance card eventually. You can ride with us or follow in your own car. It's up to you."

Addie turned back to her aunts. "I'll follow the ambulance in my car. You two stay here and wait for me." She could see their rising alarm at this suggestion. "Oh, come on. We'll all go." It was probably better to keep them with her until things got sorted out. They still didn't know how Mr. Barker died.

An efficient crew met them at the hospital. Mr. Barker was whisked one way through the emergency entrance and Addie and her aunts were led in the other direction to an intake station and presented with a clipboard holding a patient information form.

"You'll need to fill out this form and attach the patient's insurance card," directed the admissions clerk.

Addie glanced at the extensive list and shook her head. "I don't know how much we'll be able to fill in here and I don't know anything about his insurance card. Maybe it's in his billfold?"

The clerk gave Addie a look that she decided to interpret as concern rather than exasperation.

She turned to her aunts. "Helen, Rose, you'll have to help with this form."

Rose took the clipboard and filled in Mr. Barker's name and then stopped. "Oh dear, I don't know what else to put. Should I put our address? I'm not even sure how old he is. Helen, maybe you should do this."

Helen took the papers and looked at them with dismay. "Oh, I don't know anything either. I can fill in male and white, unless you think he might be other white?"

Addie took the clipboard, looked at the remaining questions and shook her head. There wasn't anything there that she could answer either.

"I'm sorry," she said as she handed the form back to the secretary, "this is all we know."

"You don't know his address?" There was a definite note of skepticism in the woman's voice.

"He rented a room at our house so we can use our address, but he was only there a few days each month. Maybe he had a more permanent address... but we can use ours," Addie finished lamely.

At that moment a young man in green scrubs appeared at the door of the office. "I'm very sorry, but we haven't been able to revive the patient."

"Oh!" was the only thing Addie could think to say. The three women looked at each other and then back to the medic.

"What happens now?" asked Addie.

"We'll have to perform an autopsy to determine the cause of death. It appears to be a heart attack, but the hospital is required to make sure," said the young man. "When we've completed that we can release the body to his family. That's you?"

"Oh my," said Rose. "I'm afraid that we don't know if he has any family or not." She looked worriedly at Helen. "Dear, did he ever mention family to you?"

"No, never," said Helen. "He never mentioned anyone. I supposed that he didn't have any family. Maybe he had friends," she added helpfully.

"Well, that looks like us at the moment," said Addie. She turned back to the woman at the desk who was scowling by this time. "So, what happens now?" Had she just asked that?

Helen and Rose were quiet as Addie drove back home from the hospital. It was long past dinner when they got home, but no one had much of an appetite.

"Oh, I feel so bad for the poor man," said Helen. "He was always so polite and thoughtful. Why, just yesterday he insisted on cleaning his own room. He said that he didn't want to put me out with dusting all of that woodwork in there."

"I think that woman at the hospital thought we were leading her on when we said that we didn't know anything about his family or friends," said Rose. "It was as if we were trying to get away with something!"

"Well," said Addie, "you'll have to admit it looks pretty odd to say that we've known the man for more than twenty years, but know nothing about him. You really don't have any idea who we can contact?"

"No, dear," said Helen. "He never talked about anything personal. He would just talk about the latest plumbing fixture, if you could get him to talk about anything at all."

"Yes, he was certainly close mouthed," added Rose. "But we always thought it was better that way. He was pleasant and paid his rent on time. I'm sure if we'd known that he was going to drop dead we would have asked him more questions."

"I guess it will be alright for us to look through his papers to see what we can find," said Addie as she started up the stairs.

"You go ahead dear. Rose and I will get a little supper ready for all of us. I'm sure we could use it."

The lights were still blazing upstairs from when they had all rushed out in such a hurry to the hospital. Addie looked around the room and wondered where to start. There weren't many personal possessions lying around. His carpentry case was open on the table and one of the tools was next to it. She picked it up and put it back into the case. She couldn't see anything in the case but tools. She closed it and snapped the latch. She turned her attention to the dresser and began opening the drawers. It made her uncomfortable to be picking through his things, but there was nothing to find. No letters, no address book. His wallet, which was in the top dresser drawer, had a drivers' license with their address, of all things. There were some coupons, but no credit cards or any other type of card. There was cash but not a lot. She tackled his suitcase, which was in the closet, but it was empty, the contents either in the drawers or hanging up. She found a small sketchbook on the nightstand together with a charcoal pencil and a nature book devoted to desert flora and fauna. She flipped through the pages of the sketchbook and was surprised at how detailed the drawings were. But there was nothing else, except the crossword puzzle lying on the floor next to the chair. It was truly amazing. There was nothing of the man to be found.

There was a knock at the front door early on the morning after Mr. Barker's burial. Addie opened the door to find she was looking at a proffered police badge in the hand of an older man.

"Sorry to bother you so early," he said. "We're investigating a murder that may have happened here in the area and I'd like to ask you a few questions."

Addie could feel her mouth go dry and her heart start racing, but before she could answer the police officer went on. "We understand that a man named William Sample does gardening work for you. Is that right?"

"Oh land sake! Has Mr. Sample been murdered?" By this time Helen was at the door and Rose was close behind her.

"No ma'am. He's not the victim. But it's likely that the victim was transported to the city dump in Mr. Sample's truck. We're checking his route that day and your house was one of his work stops. In fact, it was the last stop."

"You don't think Mr. Sample's the murderer do you?" Rose exclaimed. "We've known him for years. He wouldn't hurt a fly!"

"No ma'am, we've just started our investigation, but it doesn't seem likely that Mr. Sample's the perpetrator. The victim was from out of town, Las Vegas, and there doesn't seem to be any connection to William Sample. We just need to trace Mr. Sample's movements that day. That's why I'm here."

"What day was it," asked Addie. She was beginning to feel better about this police visit.

"Last Tuesday," answered the detective causing Addie to feel worse. That was the same day Mr. Barker died.

"Well, isn't that funny," said Helen. "That's the same day Mr. Barker died. It isn't Mr. Barker you're talking about, is it?"

"Barker?" The officer looked puzzled. "No not Barker. The victim's name was Crespi."

Addie spoke quickly to the officer. "I'm sorry. We just had a friend die and he's on our minds." She hoped that didn't sound too lame.

"Sorry for your loss ladies. I just need to know if Mr. Sample was here on Tuesday. If so, what time did he get here? When did he leave? If you could answer those questions it would be helpful."

"Oh yes, he was here Tuesday," volunteered Helen. "He came around three o'clock to clear out the poison ivy down at the back of the yard and trim some of the trees."

"Do you know what time he left?"

"No...I can't say that I do. He was still working at four when I left to go to the store, but his truck was gone when I got back at five."

"You're sure about that?" The detective was making notes in a small book.

"Yes, I remember. I thought he would still be here when I got back from the store and I could pay him for his work then." Helen paused for a moment. "That's when I went up to ask Mr.

Barker if he wanted to have dinner with us." She looked as if she might cry.

"Now, Helen, that doesn't have anything to do with Mr. Sample," Addie quickly interjected. She needed to head off this turn in the conversation. This was making her nervous. They were talking too much. "Just how was he killed?" she asked thinking of the errant bullet.

"He was shot," answered the detective.

"Shot?" from all three.

"Well, in a way. It appears that he was hit with a nail. Right between the eyes."

"Oh, my lands!" exclaimed Helen.

"Well, how on earth is that possible?" questioned Rose. "Who would put up with someone trying to kill them with a nail?"

"Well, it wasn't just a hammer and a nail," said the detective. "It was what you might call industrial strength. The nail was quite large and it penetrated his skull with a lot of force. So it had to come from a nail gun used in construction. That's why we don't believe the gardener did it. The only tools that he has are garden equipment. We've checked them out."

"Who *do* you think did it?" asked Addie and was annoyed that her voice sounded so high pitched.

"We don't have any clear leads at this time." The detective shut his notebook and slipped it back into his pocket. "We're just checking out all information."

"I don't think we've been very helpful," ventured Addie.

"Oh you never know. We gather all of the little details and they end up helping to make a big picture. I don't have any other questions today, ladies, but I may be back if something else turns up."

That's what Addie was afraid of.

Addie had hurried Rose out of the house and down to the store to open by ten. She didn't know why she hadn't mentioned Mr. Barker's tool kit when she'd learned how Crespi had been killed. But she hadn't. What was going on? Mr. Barker was the most mild-mannered individual she had ever met. Maybe there was no connection, but maybe there was. What did they really know about him? Even though he had rented a room from her aunts for more than twenty years, they didn't have any idea who to notify about his death. As it turned out, they couldn't even locate a work address for him. They had finally decided that they were the nearest connection he had to a family and accepted the responsibility of a funeral and burial for him. There was an extra spot in their family plot so they used it for Mr. Barker. And they paid the hospital expenses.

There were several customers waiting at the door of the shop and Addie remembered that this was the first day of their summer sale. She and Rose bustled about turning on the lights, encouraging the shoppers to take their time, setting out some lacy linens just in from the market, not on sale, of course, and launching another day full of hope for the little store. Before she knew it lunchtime was upon them and Rose went to the back of the store for her usual cup of tea and ham sandwich. Addie was just beginning to think about her own lunch, and marveled that she hadn't thought about Mr. Barker since they had come into the store, when the door opened and there was Michael Kahn with a large shipping box in his arms.

"Hi, Addie," he smiled. "I hope I'm not getting you at a bad time." He paused expectantly.

"Oh...no, not at all." The earring display case! She'd forgotten all about it. Her mind went directly to the balance page of the store's bank account.

"It came in this morning so I wanted to bring it right over. I can help you set it up and it should help those earring sales."

"Wow, thanks! Say...listen, I'm sorry about your invoice. I know it's overdue. I feel terrible about making you wait for your money."

"No, really, don't worry about it," he said. "I take it as a positive sign."

"Positive sign?" Addie was confused.

"Sure. I figure it means you're not trying to get rid of me. Otherwise you'd have paid me off and sent me on my way." He was busy ripping open the packing box and pulling the glass case out of its wrappings.

Addie laughed. "Well, there's an excuse I haven't used on the bill collectors."

"Yeah, I'm an optimistic guy. I try to see the positive side of every situation." He was smiling as he set the assembled case on the counter. "Speaking of optimism. I was wondering if I could take you to lunch." He noted Addie's brief hesitation and added, "Don't get me wrong. You'll still owe me for the evening bags."

She laughed again, "Well, that's a relief!"

Just then Aunt Rose popped out from the back room.

"Oh, hello Michael. I didn't hear you come in. Oh look at the nice display case!" She had just spotted the glass case. "Oh that's just handsome! The earrings will do well in that."

"I'm glad you like it," he answered but Aunt Rose was already on to another subject.

"Addie, did you remember that I have a doctor's appointment this afternoon?"

"Oh," Addie tried not to let the disappointment show. "I forgot. Don't worry, just leave when you have to." She turned to Michael, "I'm sorry."

"Hey, wait. Don't forget the positive. How about dinner instead?"

"Ok! You're on. When?"

"Tonight?"

"Great."

Addie was surprised at how much she was looking forward to this dinner date, never mind that she hadn't been out socially since she had come back to live with her aunts. There just hadn't been much time left over from the tyranny of running a small business that operated on an incredibly small profit margin, with the loss column threatening to take over at any time. She had showered and dressed and was ready with time to spare. She decided to take another look at Mr. Barker's room while she waited for Michael.

It was so odd. There was really nothing personal in the room that gave any clue to the man. Besides a few articles of clothing, there was just his tool chest...containing a very large gun looking tool of some sort. Was it a nail gun? He had spent years paneling the room with a rich oak wainscoting, one panel at a time until the project was completed just this year. He had announced it to all of them in his quiet way one morning when the ladies were at breakfast.

He rarely joined them at any meal, but that morning he had taken a cup of coffee and then rather shyly said, "Ladies, it's finished. I'd like to show it to you."

Well, of course they wanted to see it. They had all trooped up the stairs and down the hall. You could see the pride in his face. After all, he had been working on this for a long time.

The ringing doorbell brought Addie back to the present, and she headed downstairs. She was disappointed when she opened the door to find the police detective instead of Michael. What was he doing here again?

"Sorry to bother you," he began brusquely. "I hope I haven't disturbed your dinner." His tone didn't really sound like he was sorry.

Addie stepped back to let him in. "No, it's fine. Come in."

As the detective was coming through the doorway, Michael appeared on the porch behind him. He was slightly surprised to see another man at the door, but followed him inside at Addie's urging.

"Detective Jacobs?" Addie ventured. "I'd like you to meet Michael Kahn."

The detective stuck out his hand and grabbed the one Michael proffered, giving him the once over. "Glad to meet you. It's Jacobson."

"Oh sorry," Addie murmured. "Come in," she said to the detective again, giving Michael a small smile. "Mr. Kahn and I are about to go out for dinner, but come on in." She hoped that she didn't sound too chirpy. She didn't feel chirpy. She felt nervous.

"I won't keep you," began the detective. "I just have a couple of things I'm trying to clear up about the murder last week."

"Murder?" asked Michael.

"Yes," answered Jacobson. "It's in connection to the victim in the gardener's truck. I just have a couple of questions about your boarder who died the same day."

Michael was thoroughly confused. But apparently Addie wasn't.

"Mr. Barker? He had a heart attack. You don't think there's a connection do you?" She felt like biting her tongue. Why did she suggest that?

"Not really, but it did seem like an odd coincidence. How long did he live here?"

Just then Aunt Rose appeared from the back hall, "Oh, Mr. Barker was with us for the last twenty years," she volunteered. "He was just the sweetest man."

"Yes, ma'am, I'm sure he was. Did he have family? Do you know who his employer was?"

This was getting to Addie. They didn't have answers to either of those questions and she knew that would sound fishy. She should just show the detective Mr. Barker's carpentry kit and get it out in the open.

"He sold plumbing fixtures," she said instead. "He was so shy. He just never really shared personal information."

"You had him buried in your family plot?"

"Well, of course we did," said Rose "I don't think the poor man had any family. In all the years he was with us he never mentioned anyone. I think he must have considered us his family."

"Oh, yes, we were certainly his family," added Helen. And then to everyone's discomfort, she started weeping. "I just wish we had been able to do more for him."

"Well, thanks ladies," said Detective Jacobson. "I don't think there's anything here to pursue. It was just that this is the only stop the gardener made that day that had anything out of the ordinary happen. I just wanted to cover all the bases."

Addie could see that Helen's tears were making the man uncomfortable. Good. He should go. She didn't know why she hadn't said anything about the tools, but now it was too late. He should just go.

He flipped his notebook shut and put it back in his pocket. "Sorry to have bothered you." He gave Michael another once over and then headed out the door.

Addie hoped that she didn't look as anxious as she felt as she reached for the glass of wine and took a sip. She and Michael had left for the restaurant a few minutes after the detective departed. She had introduced him to her Aunt Helen and then ushered him out of the door before Aunt Rose could get hold of him. She had no idea what Rose might say since she knew Michael and might feel comfortable telling him the whole story. She was still slightly shocked at her own reluctance to mention the tool chest to the detective.

"A penny for your thoughts," said Michael, adding, "although it looks like they might cost more than that." He was holding the menu in one hand and his own glass of wine in the other.

"Oh, sorry," Addie said a little embarrassed that she had been caught drifting. "You might be right about the cost. I don't think a penny is going to cover it."

"So, would I be prying if I asked about that policeman at the house?"

"No, no!" Addie assured him. "I don't mind telling you. It's a rather bizarre story."

"I don't mind bizarre," replied Michael. He had reached for the wine bottle and was starting to refill her glass.

Addie hadn't realized how fast she had finished the first one. *He'll think I'm a lush if I don't slow down,* and then said aloud, "It's been such a strange week. We just buried a man in our family plot that is turning out to be a total stranger. Then we've had the police asking about our gardener because they found a body in the back of his truck. Seems he was probably killed with a nail gun, but they have no idea where."

"Alright," said Michael, "that's definitely a bizarre story. Just what do you mean they don't know where? Who was killed? The gardener?"

"No, that was confusing, I know. But, I'm telling you, this whole week has been confusing. No, the gardener wasn't killed. A man named Crespi who came from Las Vegas ended up in the back of our gardener's truck and he was discovered when the truck was emptied at the landfill. It seems that our house was the last one on the gardener's route that day."

Addie paused and took another drink.

"Is that who you buried?"

"No. We buried a little man who has rented a room from my aunts for more than twenty years. He died that same day from a heart attack. We buried him," she repeated taking another sip.

"And this is the total stranger?" Addie noticed that Michael was refilling his glass.

"Yes, it's just so odd. You can be around someone for a long time and you think that means you know them, but you really don't." She paused for a moment and then went on. "His name was Samuel Barker and he began renting a room in our house more than twenty years ago. He only used the room one weekend a month and then for another week in the summer. Maybe in the beginning my aunts wondered about him, but he was always quiet, polite, and he paid his rent on time. He paid for the whole month even though he was only there a few days at a time. He took his meals out and never talked much about his life. It seems he was on the road most of the time selling plumbing supplies. So, even if you could get him to talk it turned out to be about u-joint pipes and bathroom fixtures. So, no, we never really got to know him."

Just then the waiter reappeared and they took time to order. Addie was glad of the break. The more she talked about Mr. Barker the stranger the situation seemed. She was worried that she had gotten herself into some kind of bind by not telling the detective about the toolbox. Of course, no one knew that she had closed it. So how could she be in trouble?

Their dinner arrived in courses and they talked of other things and Addie began to relax and found that she really enjoyed Michael's company. By the time dessert was served, Addie had pushed Mr. Barker to the back of her mind.

"I feel like I've monopolized the conversation. What about you? Do you like working for this jewelry company?" She hoped that didn't sound too lame, but Michael didn't seem to notice.

"Hey, it's not a bad job. It helps me keep the door open, although that's probably too broad a statement, since I don't have a door yet, just a website."

"A website?"

"I design and build custom furniture."

"I'm impressed!"

Michael laughed, "Well, I'm not sure how impressive it is just yet. So far I've only sold a few pieces, but I have hopes." He stopped to wave the waiter over. "Coffee or an after-dinner drink?" he asked her.

She hesitated and then said, "Sure, how about an Irish coffee. That way I'll have both."

"Make that two," Michael told the waiter.

"I want to hear more about this furniture you build," she said as they settled back with their drinks. "Is this a hobby?"

"No, it's actually what I hope will be my life's work... as corny as that sounds. I've always liked working with my hands. I think I come by it naturally. My grandfather was a master joiner and I spent a lot of time with him in his workshop as I was growing up. I've worked in all phases of carpentry from framing houses to doing finish work inside. But my first love is building furniture. I design it, build it, and...I don't use nails," he finished with an obvious note of pride.

"Well, as I said before, I'm impressed. So how is it you're selling jewelry and ladies accessories? That seems an odd detour from you life's work."

Michael smiled, "Yes, not what anyone would think I would be doing. As I said, I've worked in the construction business, building houses mainly, and for someone else. I tried working on my own ideas with furniture design, but I was dead tired most of the time." He stopped to take a drink. "I realized that I had to free up time if I was ever going to get anywhere with a business. Of course, I still need to eat," he laughed. "So here you see me...jewelry salesman par excellence."

"Really? How does that free you up?"

"Well a lot of my time contacting new customers is spent on the phone, and store visits and cold calls can be scheduled around my time in my workshop. The other thing about it is that I'm not worn out from heavy lifting all day. So it works."

"I'd love to see what you do," said Addie hoping that didn't sound too forward. "I mean, you said you have a website. Can I see your work there?"

"Sure, but I'd rather show you in person, if you have the time."

"Yes," but Addie hesitated. This wasn't one of those offers to show her his etchings she hoped. "Yes, I have time, but probably not tonight," she finished lamely.

"No, not tonight," he smiled reading her mind. "I'd like to show you my workshop and it's sort of out in the country. How about a Saturday?"

"Ok... Saturday sounds good. This Saturday?"

"You bet! Oh, and feel free to bring your aunts."

"Ok," she laughed, "but I don't think that will be necessary. Was I being obvious?"

"Yes," he grinned.

Michael pulled up in front of her house, got out of the car, and came around to open Addie's door. "Hey, it's been a great evening," he said. "I'm looking forward to Saturday."

"So am I." She slid out of the car and took his hand as they walked up the steps to the front door. "I had a great time. Thanks for dinner and the conversation."

"Would you think it was pushy of me to ask for a goodnight kiss?"

Addie smiled. "Yes, it's definitely pushy...but then I'm the pushy type."

Chapter 4

Las Vegas

Max Grenwald made his way through the maze of slot machines and roulette tables in a cavernous room that existed in a perpetual twilight state. There were no windows, no clocks, nothing to signal to the gamblers that time was passing. The rhythmic clanging of the slots conjured visions of silver coins pouring over a waterfall and straight into Max's bank account. He loved that sound. He loved the devotion of the old ladies who pumped those silver coins into the slots, wearing thin white cloth gloves to keep the coins from blackening their hands. Filthy lucre. It made him smile. He crossed through the door marked Private and strode down the hall to his office. He looked forward to getting the business day under way. The first item on his agenda was a report on the profit and losses of the day before. Recently the profits had been picking up from the slump that had occurred after the president admonished everyone to save money and avoid Vegas. What a schlemiel! He was killing jobs with talk like that! This casino alone had to let a fourth of the staff go; dealers, wait staff, cooks, dishwashers, maids, and on and on. Every casino in town had the same problem. The economy was in the toilet here. But POTUS had backed off after he got the word from a few of his big donors and things were starting to pick up. Max circled his desk, eased himself into his big leather chair, and buzzed Charlie Black to come in. Charlie handled the day-to-day minutia involved in the process of running one of the biggest casinos in the world. He was one of those multi-tasking wonders who could juggle dozens of issues without letting any one item get away from him. Today he looked worried.

"Charlie, you don't look so good. You coming down with something?" Max worried about his own health so he was naturally concerned about Charlie. If Charlie was coming down with something he could catch it too.

"No," said Charlie. "I'm fine." He knew what Max was driving at. He'd worked with him long enough to know that he was worried about germs, not Charlie. "A situation has come up and I'm just wondering if there is anything to worry about."

"What? Worry about what?"

"It's Harry Crespi."

"Who's Harry Crespi?"

"He works in collections. You'd remember him if you saw him, a heavy set individual, sweats a lot."

Max gave an involuntary shudder. He was fastidious himself and didn't like to be around those who had issues with personal hygiene. "So what's the matter with Harry?"

"Seems he's dead," said Charlie matter-of-factly. "Murdered."

"Well, that's awful. Not here in the casino I hope."

"No, he was in Kansas City. Don't ask me why. We didn't send him there." The casino sent Harry and his ilk out to collect on non-payment of gambling debts. It always amazed Charlie, who was not a gambler, how people could dig themselves into such a deep pit. Most of these people that they had to track down fell into the category of never having heard of the phrase *cut your losses*. Their mantra seemed to be *if you're losing, keep on throwing good money after bad.* The majority of the bad debt bunch paid up when someone like Harry showed up. They got the message right away and squared up their accounts in a very businesslike manner. But there were a few who had to learn the hard way. Nobody liked to talk about it, but debts had to be paid, one way or another. Then Harry had to collect in less conventional ways. It was hard on the poor jerks that fought the system, but it served as a good lesson to others.

"So how did you get this news?"

"I got a call this morning from the police there. They were checking into Harry's background and they found us through his insurance card."

"Insurance!" Max snorted. "The guy carried insurance?" It seemed ironic that guy in his line of work carried insurance.

"Yeah, he had the medical plan through the casino. They could track him that way."

"I don't like that he can be linked to us. It's not good for business." Max had spent his life in the business and he knew what was good for it and what was not. Their clientele liked the thrill of rubbing elbows with the rich and famous and they didn't mind if they were tinged with a Mafia aura. In fact, that made it even better. But they would not like rubbing elbows with the likes of Harry Crespi. They wouldn't like knowing that the Harry Crespis of this world, who did the dirty work for the industry, might come in contact with them, even in a figurative manner of speaking. And the industry didn't want them to hold back in their enthusiasm to throw their money after the dice by the fact that they might one day have a Harry Crespi knocking on their door.

"What happened to Harry?"

"According to the detective that I talked to this morning, Harry was killed by a shot between the eyes from a nail gun."

"You're kidding!" Max said unbelieving.

"No, he said that it was an industrial strength nail gun, but a nail gun nevertheless. They found his body in a recycling dump and haven't a clue who did it." Charlie paused. "They wondered if we could give them any leads."

"What did you say?" Max was beginning to get agitated about this whole thing.

"I said no, of course. Which is the truth. I have no idea what he was doing in that part of the country. He wasn't doing any work for us. I *would* have said that he was on vacation, but I don't think he would know how to act on a vacation. He was obviously on his own doing what he does best."

"What would that be?"

"Terrorizing someone, of course. Looks like it backfired on him."

"So are we going to hear more from this detective?"

"I doubt it, but I'll let you know if we do." Charlie turned to leave the office and then turned back. "Oh, I almost forgot. The accounting department called my office wondering if we had heard from George Cravetz."

"Who the hell is George Cravetz?" Max was beginning to lose patience. Who were these people?

"He works for us in accounting."

"Never heard of him."

"He's been in accounting for almost forty years." Charlie knew everybody that worked for the casino, unlike Max who concentrated on the clientele to the exclusion of the hired help. "Well, he hasn't come to work for the last two days and he hasn't called in. His office is concerned."

"Two days?" Max was skeptical. "Why would they be worried after only two days?"

"It seems it's out of character for him. He hasn't missed any work in the past forty years. He takes a one-week vacation each year and that's it. His office called his house and no answer. So they're asking us."

"They should call the hospitals." Max was ready to be finished with this topic. He had better things to do. "Maybe you should check the books," he added as an afterthought.

"You might be right about that," agreed Charlie. "I'll go over to accounting and see what else I can find out."

Max nodded and gave himself a mental pat on the back. He had to think of everything.

Charles Black graduated from the Sloan School of Management at MIT with an MBA. He was one of the brightest in his class. He worked for a short period as a consultant with a financial institution but found the work unchallenging. A chance invitation to a dinner party as an extra man changed the course of his career. That evening he met, and then eventually married, the niece of a man who had created a gambling empire. He had casinos on both coasts and in-between, among various other enterprises. Charlie had impressed the uncle with his business knowledge and was pleased when he was offered the position of assistant business manager at the Las Vegas casino, and, while the marriage hadn't lasted, the job did.

In the five years that he had been here he had learned every aspect of the business, unlike Max, who was relieved to turn over the headaches of management to Charlie and concentrate on the glam of taking care of the high rollers. Max might not have had so much faith in Charlie if he knew who his connections were. Charlie knew that the corporate office still had their eye on him even though his domestic situation had changed, and he knew that he could one day take over the entire operation at this casino, if he played his cards right. Max was just a placeholder in Charlie's mind. But Charlie also knew that his connections didn't look kindly on mistakes that caused a reduction of the bottom line. So he made it his business to know everything that went on. Which is why he was already checking the books. He opened the door to the accounting department and went in.

"So, how do they look?" he asked as he sat down in the chair next to the desk of Tom Woods, second in seniority in the department.

"Everything's in order," answered Tom with a slight shrug of his shoulders. "George is meticulous. Nothing out of line in his bookwork, and his money delivery to the Midwest is, and always has been, faultless." He shook his head as he thought about George. As an accountant himself, he was orderly and methodical, but George took it to another level. He never wavered from the rituals of his daily, weekly, yearly routines. From the turkey sandwich on whole wheat that he had day in and day out for lunch, to the yearly trek in the desert that he counted as a vacation, nothing varied. That's why Tom was concerned when George was two days late coming back from that vacation and hadn't called.

"He takes a week in the desert every year...by himself, and anything could happen to him," worried Tom. "He can't be in some hospital or they would have contacted us."

"He's got insurance, of course," confirmed Charlie. If a guy like Crespi had insurance, then this Cravetz had insurance. "Any idea where in the desert he goes?" The American Desert was a large place. If a search had to be launched, it would help to narrow it down.

"Not really," Tom answered a little sheepishly. "Every year he asks around the office if anyone wants to go camping with him, but no one ever does. We're not much of a camping group." He knew that it wasn't the camping issue with the staff as much as it was spending the time with him. "I can't remember where he goes. I think it's someplace different each year. He brings back sketches, but not much else as far as where he was."

"Has anyone been out to his house?" Charlie was beginning to have a bad feeling about this. "Maybe he's dead in his house."

"That's a grim thought," said Tom. "Maybe I should take a drive by on my way home from work today."

"Never mind, I'll run by now. Just give me his address." He waited while Tom pulled up George Cravetz' file and jotted down the number and street. He put the slip of paper in his pocket and turned to go.

"Here's something you might be interested in," said Tom, looking up from the computer screen. "George is also in charge of the gold account..."

"What gold account?" This was news to Charlie. Not just that George was in charge of the gold account, but that there was a gold account at all. He was irked that he didn't know about it.

"The House has had a stash of gold in the vault for years. Every once in awhile a player wants to deal in gold. Doesn't happen very often, but we can accommodate if we need to."

"Can you get me the information on this account?" Charlie asked.

"I'll get it right away, but it's not part of our public books."

There were some financial dealings that were public knowledge to all who had the right to know, like the IRS, and then there were some things that were 'family' matters. Apparently this was one of them.

"Well, see if you can get me the file or whatever by the time I get back."

"You bet."

"And call the insurance agency. Maybe a claim has been put in if he's been injured and that might tell us where he is."

The trip to George Cravetz' house hadn't produced anything besides a feeling of depression. It was a small non-descript house in a neighborhood full of small non-descript houses. The yards consisted of sand, rocks and cacti, most likely volunteers since there was no apparent landscape plan. Charlie had rung the doorbell and, when he got no answer, knocked loudly, and then walked around to the back door and banged on it with the same result. Nothing. The garage was attached to the side of the house and had a single dusty window. When he looked in he could see that it was empty. So probably George wasn't lying dead or stricken inside. No reason to call the police out here to the house. It was casino policy, and common sense, to involve the police in company business as little as possible.

He had returned to his office to find a black leather folder waiting for him on his desk. The contents of the folder blew him away. He had no idea that the casino had such a hoard of gold. According to the ledger, there were coins and gold bars, mainly kilo bars, and there were two hundred and ninety-nine of those. A quick calculation based on the ticker price on CNBC running across the bottom of the TV in Charlie's office caused him to suck in his breath. He picked up the phone and called Accounting.

"Tom, can you come up here," Charlie paused and then added, "Bring any other info you have on this gold thing." He had a nagging feeling that somehow this was going to turn out badly for him. He cursed under his breath that he hadn't known about this gold account. But if he didn't know about it, it was highly possible that Max didn't know about it, or at least hadn't remembered it. He wouldn't say anything until he had all of the facts. He flipped through the files again for anything to report, but the gold ledger had been the main piece of information.

Tom came into the office empty handed. "I couldn't find anything else on paper," he began, "but Miss Alcott in accounting knows about the gold because it's her job to assist in the monthly audit with George." He paused and then added, "I thought you might want to go take a look."

Charlie certainly did want to take a look. He stood up, picked up the folder and followed Tom out into the hallway and down to Accounting.

"Oh yes, I know about the gold in the vault," said Mildred Alcott, who looked as if she came from central casting after a call for "typical middle-aged spinster accounting geek. "I sit in each month when Mr. Cravetz audits that account."

"This is a monthly routine?" asked Charlie Black.

"Mr. Cravetz believes in routine. He says that it is the mark of a competent bookkeeper. 'Always keep your ducks in a row' he says." She nodded her head several time to punctuate the thought.

"Are there a lot of transactions in this account?"

"No." She wrinkled her brow. "Not many of the visitors to the casino seem to want to use the gold, but when they do, it's here. I once asked Mr. Cravetz why we didn't just check it when there was a transaction. All he said was 'ducks in a row.'" She thought a moment, "Mr. Cravetz believes in routine. He says it keeps mistakes from happening. He has to double-check the cash that he transports to the investors each month and I think he just makes checking the gold account part of the routine. It's in the same vault, you see."

Charlie Black knew that all cash business in the casino back office was checked and double-checked with security guards present. No point to make things easy for a thief.

"So, you and Mr. Cravetz check these two accounts together, and security is present?"

"Yes sir!" Miss Alcott declared. "If security isn't there, I'm sure Mr. Cravetz will request them. He always says that you have to be scrupulously careful when you are dealing with other peoples' money."

"I'd like to see the gold."

"Yes, of course." The woman opened a desk drawer and took out a black folder similar to the one Charlie was holding. "I have my part of the combination here. You'll need Mr. Cravetz' part to open the safe."

"Where would I find that?"

"It should be in that folder you're holding," said Mildred Alcott. "It's the one that he always brings with him."

Charlie flipped open the file, not sure where to look. There were accounting sheets and memos and a small envelope taped to the inside cover. He lifted the flap and retrieved a slip of paper.

"That's it," said the bookkeeper, and then hesitantly, "Do you mind if I ask if we've found out where Mr. Cravetz is?"

"No, we haven't heard anything yet, but I'm sure he's fine," Charlie assured her. "He just has to miss a few days of work, that's all." No need to start rumors he thought.

Miss Alcott shook her head in a worried way. "Well, that's just not like him. He's never missed a day of work since I've been here, and that's sixteen years." She would have asked more questions, but the look on Mr. Black's face deterred her. She stood up and led the way to the main vault. It looked like a vault that you would find at a bank, and, in fact, it was a bank vault. The casino dealt in large sums of cash, and security was always a priority. There were two security guards at the entrance and another at a desk just inside.

"Good morning, Sam," Miss Alcott greeted the sitting guard. "This is Mr. Black from the head office. We want to get into the safe with the gold."

"Without Mr. Cravetz?" said the guard rising from his chair.

"Without Mr. Cravetz," said Charlie Black. "Just Miss Alcott and me today, Sam."

The security guard raised his eyebrows momentarily then reached for his keys and led them back into the belly of the vault. There was a small cubicle behind a gated opening. Inside there was a large safe and a tall table. It reminded Charlie of the safety deposit vaults at regular banks. The guard unlocked the gate and Miss Alcott proceeded to the safe.

"You put in your part of the combination first and then I'll put in mine."

He took the slip of paper out of the folder and put in his portion and then stood back.

"Ok, your turn."

She hesitated for a moment. "Mr. Cravetz always insists that we turn our backs when the other one is putting in their part."

"Don't worry, Miss Alcott I won't peek." She looked doubtful. Maybe it didn't occur to her that he could just take her part of the code if he felt like it.

Miss Alcott stepped up to the lock and without looking at the slip of paper in her hand, finished the combination. She pulled the handle and the door swung open and the gold lay before them. There were several large bars, stacks of kilo bars and plastic sleeves containing coins. There was a lot of money.

Charlie turned to Miss Alcott. "What do you do now?"

"Mr. Cravetz takes all of the gold bars and coins out of the safe and puts them on the table and then we count them." She was beginning to feel very nervous. "You'll find an inventory sheet in there," she said nodding toward the file in Charlie's hand.

"Ok," he said locating the sheet. "Let's count." He turned toward the guard. "What do you do while they are counting, Sam. It is Sam, isn't it?"

Sam nodded, "Yes sir. I stay right here while they count. Mr. Cravetz insists. He always says we can't be too careful with other peoples' money." He was beginning to be uneasy about all of this. "They always count the cash in the travel bag at the same time, but it's not the right time of the month for that now."

"Yes, I know," said Charlie. "We'll just count the gold now anyway," and he began stacking the piles on the table.

Later, when they had finished, Charlie was surprised to see that the amount on hand checked out. He wasn't sure what he would find, but he wasn't expecting this. There were various denominations of gold coins from varying nations enclosed in their own plastic sleeves. The kilo bars were in stacks of ten, six rows by five deep. One stack had only nine bars, but everything was there according to the ledger.

Miss Alcott was obviously relieved. "Mr. Cravetz is just meticulous," she said.

Sam, the security guard, was puzzled. What was going on? He'd watched this process month after month over a number of years and it had never occurred to him that there was anything wrong with the procedure. And where was Cravetz? He must have dropped dead if he wasn't there at work.

Charlie began stacking the golden horde back on the cart. Something was wrong but he couldn't put his finger on it. He looked down at the two bars he was holding, one in each hand. Was it his imagination, or was there a difference in them. They were both marked the same and they were the same denomination. He hefted each and, again, wondered if it was his imagination, but the weights seemed different.

"Miss Alcott, I'm going to check out these two bars. Do you have any kind of a sign-out sheet?" It sounded like he was at the library checking out books.

"Well...no official sheet," she answered, "but we could write it down on a piece of paper...and all sign it. Would that be alright?"

"That's alright by me," said Sam. "Besides, Mr. Black, you're the boss."

"You're right about that, Sam," answered Charlie as he pocketed the bars and signed the paper, which was placed in the safe with the rest of the gold and locked up with it.

So now he knew what was wrong. Charlie Black stared at the report from the assay that he had had done on the two bars. He was right about the weight. One was lighter than the other. But the big news was that while one was 999.9% pure gold, the other was a clever imitation, a lead bar covered with a shiny gold coating. Very well done, very difficult for the average person to detect, very disturbing.

He had a sinking feeling that this wasn't the only bad bar in the batch. How long had Cravetz worked for the casino? Long enough to switch a lot of good bars for bad. It had to be Cravetz. Maybe the other two were in on it, but it didn't seem likely. Cravetz was a loner and a man of mind-numbing routine. And now his routine was broken. Two more days had gone by and George Cravetz had not returned. Charlie knew that he should report this up the chain. But he also knew that the news wouldn't be taken well. Better to find out what was going on first. He needed to see the gold again, but without Miss Alcott, or the regular guard. If there was a problem, he didn't want them to know, not yet. He didn't want rumors flying.

The phone rang and Charlie answered to hear his secretary say that the head office in Philadelphia was on the line. He picked up and found himself talking to Frank Watson, assistant to the CEO of the Casino Corporation. This same CEO, John Giamacchi, was his former uncle by marriage, the man who brought him into the business.

"Charlie, Frank Watson," the voice declared.

"Frank! Great to hear from you!" He hoped that was true. "What can I do for you?"

"I'll get right to the point, Charlie. We've scheduled a job performance review for you and want you to come back to Philly. See the big boss."

"Say, that's great." Charlie had had these reviews before but they had always taken place right here in Las Vegas. What was up with this? "When do you want me there?"

"Right away, Charlie. No point to let grass grow, as they say. See if you can get back here tomorrow. I know that's a tall order."

"Ok, I'll get right on it."

"And Charlie, keep this to yourself. There's some reorganization going on. We don't want the word out too soon."

"You can count on me, Frank. I'll be there tomorrow."

"That's good, that's good. Take care of yourself Charlie."

"You bet." The call was over. Charlie's mind was racing. Reorganizing! What did that mean? Was he getting a promotion? Why else call him all the way back to the head office. His thoughts returned to the problem at hand, the missing gold. He realized if it became known that the Casino had taken a hit right under his nose, there would be no promotion, probably no job, and that was the best-case scenario. He would have to find out how much gold was missing and then find George Cravetz. He would start looking as soon as he got back.

Chapter 5

Philadelphia

Charlie Black walked out of the Philadelphia Airport terminal and got into the taxi line. He had not arranged for a private car service because he didn't want to see his name prominently displayed by the drivers picking up passengers. His instructions had been to come east without a lot of fanfare. The ride into Philly where the corporation headquarters were located was stop and go in the midday traffic and Charlie was breaking a sweat, partly from the heat and humidity, and partly from nervous anticipation. He had a long time on the flight to think about what he was walking into and, for the most part, it seemed promising. He knew that his job performance was top notch, so what else could it mean to come back here for the review other than a promotion. He was ready for it, too. He was ready to step up to Casino boss. The question was, which casino? There were a number of them in various parts of the country and any one would work out for him. He had no ties to Las Vegas.

He had also had time to think about the gold situation. He decided not to say anything now. It was a topic that could kill any promotion deal. He felt sure that George Cravetz was responsible and he would track him down. If he couldn't find him, then he would ostensibly make the discovery at that time that the gold had been switched. But it would be better to find him.

Frank Watson's secretary escorted him right into Frank's office. "He's expecting you, Mr. Black. We appreciate you letting us know when you would arrive."

Frank stood up as Charlie came in and stuck out his hand. "Great to see you, Charlie. How was the trip?"

"Smooth, Frank. Thanks for asking. It gave me some time to get a little reading done. For a change."

Frank waved him into a chair across from his desk. "Sit down, Charlie. Let me give JG a call and see if he's ready for us." He picked up the phone and inquired. "His secretary says come on up. By the time we get there we can go in."

Charlie was feeling better about this all the time. A person at his level in the company wouldn't see the CEO to get bad news. Frank Watson would have handled that.

They entered the large reception area of the executive offices. It smelled of money: dark wood paneling; plush sofas; extravagant arrangements of flowers; and executive secretaries waiting to greet them. A striking blond woman, impeccably groomed, stood up when they came in.

"Hello Frank. It's nice to see you Mr. Black. Mr. Giamacchi is ready for you, just follow me."

She ushered them into the CEO's office, which might have been even larger than the reception area they just came from. It, too, was paneled, on three walls, with rich looking polished wood and displayed some impressive artwork. Charlie wasn't an art critic, but one of them looked like a Picasso. The fourth wall was all glass with a spectacular view of the city and the bay. John Giamacchi, sitting behind a desk that could have doubled as a small stage, stood up as they came in, laid the large cigar that he had been nursing in a crystal ashtray and came around the desk.

"Charlie! Good of you to come." He glanced at his secretary, "Hold my calls Phyllis. I'll let you know when we're through." She nodded her understanding and retreated out of the office closing the door behind her.

"You're looking good Charlie. Fit. Tan. Las Vegas agrees with you." He was guiding Charlie and Frank over to a more relaxed setting with a comfortable leather sofa and chairs grouped around a large coffee table sporting what looked like a Frederick Remington bronze. He opened cabinet doors along the wall and revealed a well stocked bar.

"What can I get you? Charlie? Frank?"

"The Macallan sounds good, JG." Frank chose from a number of top shelf scotch brands on display.

"Make that two," added Charlie. He never drank at this time of the day, *but when in Rome.* It was feeling more than ever like a special occasion.

"Good. Water? Ice?"

"Not for me," answered Frank.

"Same here," chimed in Charlie.

Giamacchi delivered the drinks to the men, poured one for himself, retrieved his cigar and then sat down with them. "I'll get right to the point, Charlie." He took a deep pull on the cigar and let the smoke curl up toward the ceiling. "There are a lot of changes about to take place in the organization and I want to let you in on what's happening."

Again Charlie felt encouraged.

"And, as the saying goes, there's good news and bad news. The bad news for the corporation is that we're losing money on the Atlantic City casino and we're going to pull out of there."

"Sorry to hear that." Charlie wondered how that affected him.

"But the good news is that we've got some plans in the making that will expand our business more than ever. What it means," JG went on, "is that there is going to be a lot of reorganization. We're going to be shifting personnel."

"I see," nodded Charlie, although he didn't see...yet. "Will this affect me?"

"Yes, but it shouldn't be much of an adjustment. Frank, get me Charlie's folder there on my desk."

Frank obliged and then sat down again.

"We've got a good report on you here, Charlie," he was leafing through Charlie's file. "Frank tells me that you've made a difference in the operation in Las Vegas."

"Thanks," Charlie took another sip of the scotch.

"I don't think we're paying you enough and we're going to make that right."

"Well, that's appreciated."

"The other news, and I don't know if it's bad or good, is that we're going to let Max Grenwald go."

"Really!" Was he getting the Las Vegas casino? His heart was racing.

"Max is a good man, you understand, just not creative. Innovative. And we need someone in Las Vegas who can ramp up the operation." JG took another pull at the cigar and added, "It's not Max."

Charlie was trying not to let his excitement show. You don't want to give the impression that you're dancing on the other fellow's grave of rejection.

"Does Max know?"

"Not yet. He's scheduled to come back here next week and we'll break it to him then. We'll give him a good severance package, but that's not the kind of news you want to hear where you work. Too many people sticking their noses into things."

"I see. That could make it harder to take." Charlie almost felt compassion for Max.

"That's why we brought you back here. If one of us shows up in Vegas, all the heads start talking. Am I right Frank?" Frank nodded his agreement. "We get you here and we can get this money thing worked out with the finance office, and it gives us a chance to introduce you to your new boss."

Charlie was stunned, but he didn't flinch, in fact he took a sip from his glass. "Great," he managed to get out. "Who's it going to be?"

"Phil Barcone. He's been running the casino in Atlantic City."

"I thought you were losing money there?" Charlie couldn't help the remark.

"Oh yes, we're losing money, but it's not Phil's fault." He shook his head and tapped an ash into an ashtray at his elbow. "No, the fault lies squarely with Mother Nature. Hurricane Sandy wiped out the whole industry there. Everybody's looking to get out. Trump. Everybody." He was relighting the cigar, which had ceased to smolder. "Our hope is to beat the crowd. And we hope to get some action going elsewhere. Phil's our man. He had Atlantic City popping before the storm. Frank...see if you can get Phil up here."

"Will do, JG."

Charlie went through the motions of the introduction. He said all of the right things: "looking forward to working with you;" "anything I can do to help, just ask." He followed Frank to the payroll department and sat while the forms and papers were filled out for his raise. He thanked Frank for everything, gave the secretary a nod on his way out, caught a taxi and returned to the airport. He didn't have a reservation, but there were always flights to Las Vegas and he'd get a spot.

Christ! A raise! A goddamn raise! They brought him all the way east just to tell him that? So much for connections! Maybe he should have stayed married, because it was obvious that he was an outsider now.

His new boss, Phil Barcone, gave him an enthusiastic handshake and a few slaps on the back and said he looked forward to working with Charlie, too. And as soon as he was settled in, they'd get square on Charlie's responsibilities. First, they'd have to do some routine housekeeping: reviewing staff evaluations, doing an audit, and just make sure that everything was generally shipshape.

An audit. The gold. Charlie reclined his seat on the airplane, opened one of the two vodka mini bottles he had just purchased, he didn't like scotch, and poured it over the ice in the plastic glass. He had some thinking to do.

Chapter 6

Kansas City

Addie waited impatiently for Rose and Helen to give up their hold on Michael. He had come to pick her up for a trip to his farmhouse and workshop, but the aunties had insisted that he have a cup of coffee and a warm homemade cinnamon role, and they fussed over him like mother hens. Addie was embarrassed.

"Rose, Helen, I think Michael and I have to leave soon or we'll never get to the farm," she said with a slightly pleading tone in her voice.

"Oh Adele," chided Rose. "You have all day! You won't be late!"

Michael stood up from the kitchen table winking at Addie and said, " Aunt Rose, Aunt Helen, you've got my day off to a great start. The coffee and roll just hit the spot. But Addie's right, we should go."

Then just as Rose was about to protest, the doorbell rang.

"Well, who could that be?" Helen wondered as she stood up and headed for the front door.

They all followed her into the hallway and stood as a reception committee when she opened the door. There stood Detective Jacobson, hat in hand.

"Good morning ladies. I hate to bother you again but I have a few questions I hope you can answer. Oh sorry, it looks like you're going out," he said to Addie. She had picked up her purse and was looking anxiously from Michael to the door.

"Yes, Mr. Kahn and I were just on our way out."

"Well, this won't take long. I just want to ask again about the gentleman who lived here. You say he worked for a plumbing supply company?"

"Yes," said Rose and Helen in concert.

"Well, the odd thing is," Jacobson went on, "we haven't been able to locate a plumbing supply company that's heard of him. Samuel Barker, right?"

"That's right," said Addie. "But there must be thousands of plumbing supply companies."

"Oh, there are," answered Jacobson. "But there are ways to check. We even spread the search to the western states. Thought maybe there might have been some connection to the man who was killed the same day Barker died. Couldn't find anything."

"That man was from Las Vegas!" said Rose indignantly. "Our Mr. Barker wouldn't have any connection to someone from Las Vegas!"

"That's right!" chimed in Helen. "Mr. Barker was a gentleman."

"You know," said Addie, "we just always assumed it was a plumbing supply company."

"Yes," said Rose. "It could have been a bathroom company or the like. He always talked about pipes and connectors so we just thought of plumbing. It could have been anything!" She was starting to get a little worked up and her voice was rising in pitch.

"Yes ma'am," the detective answered. "I don't really think there's any connection, but it's just one of those odd coincidences and I like to tie things up if I can. It's just a loose end." He looked around at the little group and then gave Michael a nod. "I'll leave you with the ladies here. Sorry to have bothered you."

"Not a bother," said Addie. "Anything we can do to help." She left it at that, but had that gnawing feeling that something really was wrong. Again, she hadn't said anything about Mr. Barker's tools. She wasn't sure, but that big tool that had been beside the case was nagging at her.

"Ready?" Michael asked Addie. He had a puzzled look on his face, but brushed it aside and gave Rose and Helen a polite hug and a thank you for the breakfast treat, and then held the door for Addie.

The drive from the rush of the city into the quiet of the rolling countryside helped Addie relax and put aside the nagging uneasiness that Detective Jacobson's visit had brought up.

She was surprised at the extent of Michael's farm: the farmhouse, of course, and a number of outbuildings, and then fields of corn and soybeans.

"Do you do all of this farming yourself?" She was astonished by the thought.

"No, I don't do a bit of it," Michael laughed. "The land is rented out. I wouldn't know where to start. But the land is good so I just felt that it should have someone using it. My heart is in the workshop. It's over here. Come on." He took Addie by the hand and steered her toward one of the larger outbuildings.

The building looked like a small barn. Michael slid a large door set in an overhead track back along the face of the building. The inside seemed dark until Addie stepped inside. Shafts of light from several skylights pierced the dimness and revealed table saws and workbenches with tools neatly organized above them. Michael flipped a switch on the wall and overhead lights blazed down on the work area. Perched on a long worktable against one wall was a row of chairs, each different, each beautiful.

"These chairs are amazing!" Addie was running her hand over the beautifully turned wood, the intricate detailing and gleaming patina giving the work a depth of beauty worthy of a museum.

Michael beamed. "Thanks. I think they're good but you can be too involved to be objective. I'm counting on these chairs springing me from the jewelry and doodad business one day soon."

"I'm sure they will," Addie said encouragingly. "You've certainly got the talent! And the tools," she added looking around the barn. "Does it take all of this to make chairs?" There seemed to be a lot of equipment.

"Well, quite a bit of it is for woodworking, of course, but I've also done a huge renovation on the house. It was in pretty bad condition when I moved in. It was my grandparents' home and they died a long time back so it just sat here empty." He began turning the lights out and a quiet duskiness settled over the workroom. "Come on, I want to show you the house."

The house was a tour de force on its own. He had inherited the place from his grandfather and had spent many hours reworking the interior to bring it into this century. He removed walls, lifted ceilings, and added large mullioned windows to bring in the rolling countryside with its fields and stands of hickory and ash and walnut. The kitchen was a large open area with marble countertops and gleaming stainless steel appliances.

"Do you like to cook?" he asked.

"I've never had to do much," said Addie a little apologetically. "Aunt Helen does all of that now, and when I was living in Chicago I was usually just cooking for myself and I never put much into it. So, it's not that I don't like to cook. I just don't know how. But I love to eat?" she added with a smile.

"Good! I'm fixing lunch. And you can tell me all about Chicago."

They talked of many things over lunch: Chicago, the store, his plans for building a business, her worries about her aunts.

"The problem is," she said over a glass of wine, "is they have absolutely no money. They never worked at a job where they could earn Social Security, and certainly never worked where they might get retirement. In fact, Aunt Helen has never worked outside the house. That's why I came back from Chicago. Their only income is from the store, and that, for all practical purposes, is non-existent...and the money from Mr. Barker, who actually *is* non-existent now."

"Wow, that's a hard one," Michael commiserated. "Can they get another renter?"

"Oh yes, I'm sure they can. But that's just a stopgap measure. Eventually, they'll be too old to manage renters." She didn't add that would probably fall to her, a thought that depressed her slightly. "They will have to think of selling the house, I guess. They have taxes to pay on it now and upkeep. It's a lot of money when you don't have much." Addie paused and looked out over the rolling hills. "The thing is, they've always lived in that house, and I'd like to try and keep them there. So I'm going to make a success of this store if it kills me," she finished with a laugh.

The warm afternoon sun filtered through the trees and onto the veranda where they were sitting. A warm breeze gently brushed Addie's hair off of her neck. The mesmerizing song of the cicadas rising to a crescendo and then dropping off left her feeling strangely satisfied. She could sit here forever.

But she didn't. Standing up, she said, "Well, I'm not much of a cook, unlike you," she smiled. "That was a delicious lunch. But I have other skills. Wait until you see me with a dishpan."

Michael laughed, stood up, and followed her into the kitchen. They made quick work of the cleanup and he closed down the house.

"I hope you'll come back," he said.

Addie smiled. "I was hoping you'd say that. I love it here. I'll come back."

As they were driving back to the city, Addie asked if he would like to stay for dinner. "I don't know if you've had too much of our family today, but I'll bet anything Helen has a roast in the oven." She had seen the dinning room table already set for four with the best dishes this morning before Michael arrived.

"You bet," smiled Michael. "I wouldn't want to disappoint Aunt Helen. And besides, my cooking effort today was about the extent of my repertoire."

"Oh good." She hoped the grin on her face didn't look as goofy as it felt.

After a few minutes she added, "When we're at the house there's something I'd like to show you. It's in Mr. Barker's room, a tool of some sort. You'll know what it is, I'm sure."

Chapter 7

Las Vegas

Max Grenwald sat in his comfortable leather office chair, back to the desk, gazing out over The Strip with its garish casino lights muted by the glare of the noonday sun, and contemplated Paradise. At least it was his idea of Paradise. He had worked in Vegas all of his life, and he had started from the bottom, runner on the casino floor, then dealer, then up to management. He had such a feel for the business that the owners had taken notice and they had brought him along. In fact, he had such a feel for the business that he knew something was wrong. Why had these two individuals, this Crespi person and this Cravetz person, gone missing at the same time? Even more worrisome was the fact that Charlie Black walks in the office late yesterday and says he's taking a few days off. "Personal business." Fine. Everyone has personal business. But somehow this whole thing was making Max's palms itch. Itchy palms are supposed to mean you're getting money. But Max had always found it otherwise. He turned back to his desk, picked up the phone and called the accounting department.

Tom Woods picked up the phone. He was about to leave for lunch and crossed back to his desk to take the call.

"Accounting, this is Woods."

"Yeah, Woods. This is Max Grenwald. Upstairs." That was unnecessary information for Tom. He knew who Max Grenwald was.

"Yes sir. How can I help you?"

"I got a few question I want to ask. I'll come down," he said. Then he added, "I'm not putting you out?"

"Of course not, Mr. Grenwald. I could come up, if you want."

"No, I'd rather come down," and he hung up.

Tom looked at the clock – 11:55. "Miss Alcott you better go to lunch first today. I can go later. Mr. Grenwald's coming down about something."

Mildred Alcott was watering the office plants, her usual routine on Friday. "You don't think it's bad news about Mr. Cravetz, do you?" She looked very worried.

"He didn't say what it was about, just that he was coming down here."

"Yes...alright, I'll go on to lunch. I'm finished here." She tucked the small watering can into the bottom drawer of the filing cabinet. "You'll let me know if it's news about Mr. Cravetz?"

"Of course. Don't worry." *What's going on,* he wondered. First Charlie Black, now Grenwald. No one had paid this much attention to accounting from upstairs as long as he could remember, and he could feel his anxiety level rising. Even Miss Alcott was on edge. He sighed and sat back down at his desk to wait.

Max came in, pulled a chair up to Tom's desk and sat down. He looked around the office and then asked, "What's going on?"

The question startled Tom slightly since that was just what he was wondering. "How do you mean?" he asked tentatively.

"I mean this person Cravetz from your office ... is he still missing?"

"Yes sir, it's been a week and we haven't heard anything from him." Tom paused, and then added, "It sure isn't like him." As the days went by he was beginning to fear the worst. George could be dead in the desert.

"That's what I heard. This is the individual who takes the monthly deposit back to KC, right?"

"Yes sir."

"What about this month?"

"It's still here. It hasn't gone out yet."

"So it's not missing with Cravetz."

"Oh, no sir!" Tom was a little on the defensive for George. The guy was a nerd, but he was as honest as the day was long. Tom felt sure about that. You couldn't work with someone for all these many years and not know that.

Max reached into his coat pocket and took out a pack of cigarettes. "Mind if I smoke?" he asked looking around for an ashtray. He didn't see one but that didn't stop him from lighting up. It gave him a few minutes to think. The deposit was still here so that's not where Charlie Black went. He didn't want this Woods guy to think that he didn't know what was going on upstairs, but he was beginning to realize that he didn't. By this time Tom had provided him with a makeshift ashtray, a small dish from under the plant on his desk. Who smoked these days?

"Mr. Black usually takes care of these matters," said Max through a cloud of smoke, "but he's out of town for a few days. Did he arrange for someone to make the delivery this month?"

"No sir, we didn't talk about that at all. He was just interested in the gold account."

Goddamn! The gold account! He knew about it of course, because he was the one who dealt with the players who wanted to use it. But that was so rare that it wasn't often that he thought about it. Why was Black interested in the gold?

"So, is there a problem with the gold?"

"No sir. It's all there. Mr. Black counted it and it squared with the books."

"Black counted it?"

"Yes, that's what Miss Alcott said. I didn't go to the vault with them...but she said he counted it and everything was ok."

"Who's Miss Alcott?"

"She works here...in accounting." Tom felt uneasy. Was there a problem here? "She always accompanies Mr. Cravetz when he checks that account."

"The gold account."

"That's right. Mr. Cravetz does an accounting of the gold every month when he gets the deposit for KC ready."

"Every month? He counts the gold by himself?"

"Oh no! He always makes sure that Miss Alcott, or someone from the department is with him. And, of course, security is always there. Security is always present when money is counted."

Max nodded. Casino policy. No one was ever left alone with the money. He took another drag on his cigarette and then stubbed it out on the dish.

"The money's due to KC soon, right?"

"Yes sir, it should go today, if we stay on our regular schedule."

"So let's stay on schedule. I'll take it." He stood up to leave. "By the way, how much gold is in the vault?"

"Uh...let's see...there are two big four hundred ounce bars, two hundred and ninety-nine kilo bars, and coins. I'm not sure just how much there is in coin, but I can look it up pretty quickly."

"No, that won't be necessary right now. We can do it when we get the cash ready." Max stood up to leave. "Just how much are the kilo bars on the market right now?"

"Well, let me check where gold is trading today and I can figure that out pretty quickly." He clicked his computer over to a business page that posted running figures of all of the markets on the day.

"So right now in New York gold is trading at $1,237 an ounce, and a kilo rounds off at around thirty two ounces, so...let me see." Tom quickly pushed some numbers into a calculator and announced, "Eleven million, eight hundred thirty five thousand, six hundred and sixteen. That's today of course, a few months ago it got as high as sixteen-hundred, and last year it topped around eighteen hundred." He tapped at the calculator again. "That would be seventeen million, plus. It fluctuates. It could go down tomorrow."

Max tapped his knuckles on Tom's desk, "Thanks, yeah right, it could go down...or up. So I'll be in around three this afternoon. We'll get the KC package ready."

"Yes sir. I'll let Miss Alcott know."

Another rap of his knuckles on the desk, and Max left.

Max threaded his way through the Casino slots, back to the elevators, and up to his office. Christ! Eleven million! Something is definitely going on. Max could put two and two together with the best of them! Cravetz is missing, Charlie Black leaves town on some trumped up reason, and the sweating individual, what's his name from 'accounting,' he's dead in Kansas City. Murdered. Something is sure the hell going on.

He stopped at his secretary's desk on his way to his office. "Grace, I need a round trip flight out of here tonight to Kansas City. Can you book that for me?"

"Of course, Mr. Grenwald"

"That's good. Make the return later on Sunday."

"Will you need a hotel reservation?"

"Yeah, yeah. What've they got there?"

"The Raphael...I think you'll like it. It's small but upscale and right on the Plaza, close to restaurants."

"Good, do that," and he went on in to his office. *Jesus, eleven million!*

Just then the house phone rang. Max picked it up.

"Yeah?"

"Sorry Mr. Grenwald, but I've got an angry player down here at the cashier's cage." It was Benny, the day floor manager. "He wants to see someone upstairs."

"Sure, bring him up." This was Max's bailiwick, dealing with the customers. He could smooth over the roughest situation. Usually comping a room or tickets to a dinner show was all it took. It's what made things click around here. Happy players meant a happy bottom line. Max opened his office door and strode into the reception area ready to glad-hand the disgruntled gambler.

The elevator doors opened and Benny emerged slightly behind a red-faced individual who ignored Max's hand and walked past him into his office.

"What's going on in this place!" the man fumed.

Max looked at Benny for some sort of explanation. Benny just shrugged his shoulders and shook his head. "The guy was making a scene at the cashier's cage. Something about being taken for a ride. I just got him out of there as quick as I could before too many people could see him." He paused. "You want me to wait around?"

Max looked over his shoulder at the man storming into his office. "No, that's okay. Go back to the floor. Just make sure that security is close by."

"You got it."

Max strolled back into his office and, in his most conciliatory voice asked, "Now what seems to be the problem Mr. ...?" The man looked vaguely familiar.

"Jones!" The conciliatory tone didn't seem to be working. "Although you probably call me Patsy around here!"

"Mr. Jones, whatever it is, I'm sure we can work it out."

"Ok, work this out!" The man slapped a small rectangular gold bar down on Max's desk. Now Max remembered him. He was one of the few patrons that had asked for his winnings in gold. That was more than a year ago, maybe two or three. So what was the problem now?

"I don't know what you're trying to pull," Jones continued his rant, "but if you don't make this right I'm going to the cops! Or the feds!"

"Ok, ok, Mr. Jones. I want to help. Just tell me what the problem is." Max didn't like this. You never wanted a customer complaining to anyone, let alone the cops.

"Here's the problem," said Jones waving a paper in Max's direction. "This *gold* bar is a fake! That's what the problem is."

Max took the paper. It was an assay report. Sure enough, it said the bar was worthless.

"I want my money!"

"Of course, Mr. Jones," Max's mind was racing. "The Casino always makes good on it's debts. Now tell me again, when did you get this bar?"

"It was a couple of years ago. 2011 to be exact." Jones was calming down now that it seemed that Max wasn't going to argue. "I had a big night and I took the payout in gold. I needed some cash recently and when I tried to sell the bar they said it was fake." He pointed to the assay report. "That's what it says right there."

Max knew he could deny that the bar came from the Casino, but that would bring on another threat to go to the police. Better to pay the guy off and get rid of him. Besides another thought was beginning to raise the hackles on Max's neck. First get rid of Jones.

"Well, I don't know how this happened, but the Casino isn't going to let you take the loss. I assume you want cash, not another gold bar."

"You're damn right I don't want another bar!" Jones puffed up again. "It's not worth what it was then! I want the amount of money I won."

"Certainly, of course," Max agreed. "Now, let's see. I need to find out what the price of gold was then."

"Google it," said Jones. "You can put in the date and find out what the price was."

"Perfect," said Max and he pulled up a chart of gold prices for the past twenty years.

"There, look at the September price," Jones was leaning over his shoulder pointing to the 2011 line. I was here in September. That's my vacation time." He pulled a receipt from his pocket and handed it to Max. "You can see for yourself that's when I was here. September 23rd." Max glanced at the receipt. He could see that it was for the hotel bill, not anything to do with the gold, but he wasn't going to argue with him. He wanted to settle this matter and get Jones out of here. Happy. He had other fish to fry now.

"Mr. Jones, this is your lucky day. No argument from me about this matter. Let's just figure out how much we owe you." Max pulled a calculator out of his desk. "Now let's see, a kilo is 32 ounces," he started punching numbers in but Jones held up his hand.

"Wait a minute! It's 32.15! That makes a difference."

Max adjusted the number and came up with the result. $52,719.57. He smiled at Jones and showed him the figure. "That's what you get?" The smile was forced. This was a big damn mistake, but then...not really. The guy could have had this much cash at the time. Of course, that's saying that he really got this plug here. No way to prove it one way or another.

Jones nodded as Max pulled out a voucher book and wrote out the amount. "Just present this to the cashier and they'll pay out."

"Hey, that's mighty damn white of you Mr. ...." He hesitated. "I didn't catch your name..."

"Grenwald, Mr. Jones. Max Grenwald." He stood up and began ushering Jones toward the elevator. "Of course the Casino would like you to keep this matter quiet. You know, our reputation for honesty is very important."

"Oh, sure. I understand."

"And you can count on complimentary accommodations whenever you're with us." Max patted the man on the back as he stepped into the elevator. "We value your business and your friendship." He smiled as the doors slid closed.

Now Max knew what was wrong. He still didn't know what was going on, but he knew what was wrong. The gold.

It was after three before Max could make his way back to the accounting department. He'd had time since his encounter with the fake bar to create a variety of scenarios around the gold. None of them boded well for him. If there was a problem, it was going to fall on him. He was responsible for the damn stuff. Well, so was Charlie Black. And where the hell was he now? And this bookkeeper, Cravetz, where was he? What about the guy with a nail between his eyes? This all had to be related somehow. That is, if there was a problem with the gold. This one bad bar might be a fluke. But he doubted it, too many connections.

Max was anxious to get into the vault. He didn't plan to say anything about the fake bar to Woods. The fewer people who knew about it the better. So he wasn't sure how he was going to get a look at the gold.

Both Tom Woods and Mildred Alcott were at their desks when Max came in to accounting.

"Is this a good time to get the delivery ready?"

"Yes, sir." Tom stood up.

"Shall I go with you?" Miss Alcott seemed tentative. "Will it be our usual routine?" Then Miss Alcott solved his problem.

"Will we do an accounting of the gold, too? Mr. Cravetz always did that each month when we were verifying the deposit for Kansas City. Do you want to do that, too?"

"Yes, indeed. You bet. Let's stick to the routine."

"Of course, Mr. Black just checked it earlier this week, but it was early. We always do it the same time each month. I don't know if it makes a difference."

There it was! The connection to Black.

"Probably not. But let's do it anyway so the books are consistent. I take it there are books? Max tried not to let the anxiousness show in his voice.

"Oh, yes sir. There are books! Mr. Cravetz is a stickler for keeping meticulous records." Tom was leading the way to the vault. "I think these books go back at least twenty years. He's kept them ever since he was made head of the department."

"Twenty years," Max muttered. "Shit."

Max had to contain himself as they totaled up the Kansas City deposit and recorded every little detail. By this time Security had joined the accounting party.

"Now what?" Max asked as the deposit bundle was placed in its usual locked carrying case.

"We open up the safe with the gold," answered Miss Alcott. "Mr. Cravetz counts each bar and coin. 'You can't be too careful with other peoples' money,' he always says." She was holding up a card with a number on it. "This is my half of the combination for the gold safe. Do you have the other part?"

"I have the combination up in my office. I can go get it." Max was remembering when he had handled the transaction for the aggrieved Mr. Jones.

"You won't have to do that, sir," Tom said. "The other half of the combination is in this folder ... George's folder." He had brought the folder with him when they headed out for the vault. He handed it to Max. "There's an envelope inside with your half of the combination."

Max retrieved the paper with the numbers and executed his part on the dial. Then Miss Alcott finished it out. The door swung open and the gold was on view. The safe was a large one and the gold rested on a rolling cart covered in felt. It was a rather splendid sight. There was a block of gold bars sited to one side of the cart, two large gold bars in the center, and a tray of plastic cases holding coins on the other side. Considering it was worth millions, the block wasn't really very large; approximately twelve inches wide, ten inches high, by fifteen inches deep.

"Mr. Cravetz pulls the cart out to the table. Should I do that?" Mildred Alcott asked.

"Yes," Max nodded.

Miss Alcott rolled the cart out and over to a table where they all gathered around.

"This is the routine, exactly," she said and then she paused. "I'm not sure who should count all of this, because Mr. Cravetz always does it."

"Ok," said Max. "Why don't you do it since you know how it's done, and we'll all watch."

Miss Alcott glanced nervously at Max and then picked up one of the sleeves of coins. "We don't usually open these containers unless there has been some sort of transaction since last month. You can see through the case and tell if the correct number of coins is here. And then you record it in this book." She opened the ledger book, took a count and noted it.

"Then what?" asked Max.

"Mr. Cravetz counts each stack of bars."

"Individually?" asked Max. "Why? They're in neat stacks. Can't he just eyeball it?"

Miss Alcott shook her head. "I don't think I'm supposed to say this...he told me in confidence...he said it is one of his little pleasures. 'While I *am* careful with other people's money, at least I can hold it for a minute.' " She paused, and then added in a worried tone, "He is so meticulous about his accounting. I hope something hasn't happened to him. It's just not like him to disappear."

Max had a sinking sensation that George Cravetz wasn't the only thing to disappear. "So what does he do? Pick up each stack and count the bars?"

"Yes sir. It doesn't really take very long." The worried look on Miss Alcott's face was growing by the minute. "Do you want me to do that too?"

"No, I'll count them," Max wanted to look closer at the gold, not that he knew what he was looking at. He could feel the weight of the fake bar in his suit pocket, and he would love to take it out and compare it, but couldn't chance it. Maybe just looking at these other bars would tell him something. He separated one stack from the block and counted it out. The one thing that he did notice is that they didn't all have the same markings on them, although the figure 999.9 was the same. After counting three columns, front to back, he gave up. There were nine bars in one stack, but all the rest had ten. "This takes too long. I can see how many are here."

"Yes, Mr. Cravetz was much quicker. I'm sure it was all those years of practice."

"Yeah, I'm sure that's it." Max was positive that there were fake bars in the stack, maybe a lot of them. In any case, this meant trouble.

"So, let's lock this up and I'll sign for the deposit for KC." This money delivery to the "family" in KC had always amused him. It went to a couple of old geezers who were related to the owners of the Casino, a family that lived back east. There were always hints that the mob was involved, but Max had never let that bother him. Until now. Now he was damned bothered.

Chapter 8

Kansas City

Aunt Helen's dinner was a hit with Michael, and Addie could see that Michael was a hit with her aunts. Fortunately, he seemed pleased with their doting. Addie couldn't think of another word to describe their attentions to him. She didn't mind. The day had been the best she could remember in a long time, so everyone taking part in a mutual admiration fest seemed appropriate. They had just finished dessert when Addie remembered Mr. Barker's toolbox.

"Helen, Rose, I wanted to show Michael Mr. Barker's room." She didn't mention the tools. She had never said anything about them to her aunts. "I thought he'd be interested in Mr. Barker's project with the wainscoting."

"Oh, by all means," Rose declared. "You certainly should show him the room! After all of the effort Mr. Barker put in on those walls! It's wonderful that someone who can appreciate it can see it."

"That poor, poor man." Aunt Helen sounded as if she might cry. "Imagine all of those years, working so hard, and then dropping dead. Oh, he never even had a chance to just sit there and relax!"

"I'm sure he enjoyed the building," said Addie as she gently edged Michael away from the table and toward the hallway. "He always seemed so preoccupied with the work."

"*That* is an understatement!" laughed Rose. "He spent all of his time in that room. We never could persuade him to have a meal with us."

"Well, he missed out there," said Michael. "That was an excellent dinner. Thank you so much for inviting me. Here, let me help." Helen had started to clear the table.

"No, no absolutely not! Go see the woodwork!"

"You're sure?"

"Of course!" By this time Rose had jumped up to help and was shooing Addie and Michael out of the dinning room.

He followed Addie up the carpeted stairway, running his hand along the banister. "These old houses have such beautiful woodworking details. This banister was made for this stairway. You don't see that anymore. Everything is factory made now."

"Oh, yes," Addie laughed. "Plenty of woodwork, but minuscule closets. I don't think women owned more than three dresses when these houses were built."

By this time they were standing in front of Mr. Barker's old room. Addie switched on the overhead light and they went in.

"So, here's his project." She ran her hand lightly over one of the sections. "He spent years working on this room. He said that the room deserved paneling, that it made the room elegant."

"He was right." Michael was admiring the work. "It's very professional looking, too. He had to have some tools here to get the work done."

"Right here," Addie went to the closet and pulled out the tool chest.

"Well, a tool chest, of course, but I meant a saw table of some sort."

"I asked him about that once and he said that he just gave the measurements to the lumber yard and they cut the wood for him."

"Of course, makes sense."

"The most industrial tool he had seems to be this," Addie produced the gun-like instrument that had been haunting her thoughts for some time now.

"A nail gun," said Michael. "That would have been useful. Plenty of nailing involved in work like this."

"I was afraid that's what it was."

"Why?"

"The day that Mr. Barker died, and it *was* from a heart attack, even though at first we thought Aunt Helen had killed him, a man's body was discovered at the yard waste recycling facility."

"Wait a minute, you thought Aunt Helen killed Mr. Barker?"

"She thought she did. She'd picked up a gun in the hallway and it went off and there was Mr. Barker flat on the floor here in this bedroom. Dead. She thought she killed him." She paused and then added, "We couldn't see any blood. Well, we had to call 911, but then after the autopsy it turned out he was dead from a heart attack. Much to our relief!" Then Addie hastened to add, "We weren't relieved that Mr. Barker was dead, just that he wasn't shot."

"What about the other dead man? Does that have something to do with Aunt Helen?"

"No, there's nothing to do with Helen. But the police said that the body was dumped from a gardener's truck. We had a gardener working in our yard that day and we were his last stop, and it seems it was his truck that did the dumping. So now I'm wondering about Mr. Barker."

"Why Barker?"

"Remember? That other man was killed with a nail. Right between the eyes."

"Good god! Is this the nail gun?"

"It must be." Addie said. "How many nail guns can there be? What should I do? I never mentioned this gun ... tool to the police, and believe me, I've had plenty of chances to say something."

"Why didn't you?"

"I don't know really. I guess I thought I was protecting Mr. Barker somehow. In the first place, I couldn't imagine him doing something like that. If you'd met him you'd know what I mean. He was so polite and soft-spoken." She paused, "I guess that wouldn't rule out murder."

"No, probably not."

"But the other thing that kept me from saying something was that I couldn't imagine him having anything to do with the dead man. It seems he was some sort of thug from Las Vegas. It's really a stretch to think that he was involved with someone like that."

"So, what are you going to do?"

"I have to tell the police about this, but it worries me what they'll think. I've taken so long to say anything."

"Just say this is the first you knew about the nail gun. You were showing me his work and I was looking at his tools and commented on it. So now you're reporting it."

"Ok, that's good. And I've never said anything about this to Rose or Helen so they'll believe that story, too. I'm always afraid that somehow they'll spill the beans about the gun Helen found. We never told the police about that either."

"Why not?"

"To be honest, I forgot about that gun. When it turned out that Mr. Barker had a heart attack ... that was the end of it. Police weren't involved in that." She thought for a moment. "You know ... I don't even know what we did with the gun. The last time I thought about it was when they were carrying Mr. Barker out on a stretcher. It was on the hall table and Rose covered it up with a scarf."

Michael began putting the tool chest back in order and snapped it shut. "Do you want me to leave it here on the table?"

"No, I think I'll put it back in the closet. I'm just thinking I'll wait until Monday to report this. No point to ruin tomorrow, because I know we'll have a house full of detectives once I say something."

"If you want me to be here, I can. They'll probably want to talk to me anyway since I'm the one that knew it was a nail gun."

"Yes, please! It will make me feel a lot better."

She wondered later about this 'feeling better' notion. After all, she had been feeling ok as she dealt with the police all of this time. It made her smile.

The phone rang shortly after ten Sunday morning. It was Michael. "I hope I'm not calling too early?"

"Oh no! Up with the chickens, dressed and almost finished with the crossword puzzle, "Addie smiled. "What's up?"

"To be honest, I'm not sure what's up. It's just an idea that came to me in the middle of the night and I wanted to check it out, if that's ok."

"What's the idea?"

"Well, it seems kind of lame now, but still ... would it be ok for me to come by and take another look at Mr. Barker's room?"

"Of course! When do you want to come?"

"I can't get there until late this afternoon. I have a pair of chairs I'm delivering to an actual paying customer, but then I can get over there."

"Great. I'll see you when you get here."

He arrived at four and Addie let him in.

"You've really got me curious. What's your lame idea?" she laughed.

"I found myself thinking about the toolbox."

"The nail gun?"

"No, not that in particular, the other contents. There were the usual oddments in the bottom. You know, stray nails, wood glue, but the thing that got me thinking was a pressure latch."

"What's a pressure latch?"

"You usually see them on cabinet doors that don't have handles. You push against the door, it releases the latch, and the door opens. It's magnetic."

"And...what?"

"It's probably nothing. The latch is still in the plastic bag from the hardware store. But it just seemed odd. He was installing panels, not cabinets. I just thought I'd like to look around."

"Sure, come on upstairs."

The late afternoon sun was slanting in through the bedroom windows, casting long shadows on the rug from the imposing four-poster bed. Michael pulled the tool chest from the closet, set it on the table, and opened it up. He rummaged around in the bottom and produced a small plastic bag containing the latch.

"Here it is. Like I said, you can make a case for all of the other stuff in here because it would be useful to this work." He gestured toward the paneling. "This latch doesn't fit in."

"So, what do you think?"

"I don't know what I think." He had begun running his hands over the panels, pushing gently. Nothing happened. "I guess it's kind of crazy to think there's a secret compartment, but I can't think of another reason to have that kind of latch."

By this time he had worked his way to the corner where he knelt down. This time when he pushed on the lower corner of the panel, he got results. It swung open to reveal a grid-like network of rectangular boxes, almost like a honeycomb. In fact, a honeycomb was an apt description, one filled with honey. The afternoon sun glinted on the horde.

Addie was standing behind Michael, peering over his shoulder. "What is that? Insulation?"

"Oh, my god! No, it's *not* insulation." He pried one of the kilo bars out of its protective wooden pocket and looked closely at the markings. "I think it's gold!"

"Gold?"

"Gold. This is a kilo bar of gold." He looked back at the hidden compartment and counted. "Twenty. They all look the same. Twenty kilo bars of gold!" He sat back on his heels and whistled. "Do you know how much this is worth?"

"I have no idea." Addie was still trying to wrap her mind around the fact that the panel contained a secret compartment.

"Wait a minute," said Michael as he pulled his cell phone out of his pocket. "I think I can figure it out." He began trolling through the Internet looking for information. "Here we go. Gold closed around twelve hundred on Friday. So, let's see what that gets us." He brought up the calculator function and began putting in numbers. "A kilo weighs about thirty-two ounces, times twenty. That's six hundred and forty ounces, times twelve hundred dollars." He stared at the number. "This can't be right. Seven hundred and sixty-eight thousand?"

Addie let out a little gasp. "Do that again!"

Michael ran the figures again and got the same result. The two of them stared at each other and then back at the gold. Just then they heard Rose and Helen come in the front door.

"Hello!" Rose's voice trilled up from downstairs. "Addie, are you there?" They had just come back from some function at the church.

"Yes, yes, we're up here." She gave Michael a worried look. "They shouldn't see this," she whispered. He nodded, slipped the small bar back into its pocket, and gently closed the panel."

"Who is 'we?'"

"It's Michael and me. We're just looking at Mr. Barker's room again."

"Oh, that's nice Addie." By this time Addie and Michael were heading down the stairs.

"We're awfully glad to see you Michael, aren't we Helen?" Rose and Helen looked positively conspiratorial.

"Oh yes! This is just grand!"

Addie might have been embarrassed if she wasn't still grappling with the reality of the contents of the secret compartment in Mr. Barker's room.

"Can you stay for dinner?' Rose asked.

Michael shook his head, "I'm so sorry. I'm supposed to meet some buddies for dinner this evening."

Addie now felt she knew what the word "crestfallen" looked like. Her aunts were definitely crestfallen, and now she did feel a little embarrassed.

"Really, I wish I could stay." He looked at Addie, "Do you mind if I call later? I feel like we didn't finish our conversation."

"Of course, I'm here all evening. Night, actually."

"So, ok I'll call." He was looking a little shell-shocked, too. He opened the door and hesitated. "I could stay."

"No, it's ok. Just call later."

"Now what are you two up to," asked Rose as the door closed behind Michael.

"Definitely not what you're thinking," answered Addie as she headed for the kitchen and the bottle of Chardonnay.

Chapter 9

Max Grenwald arrived in Kansas City on Saturday afternoon. His original plan to come on Friday had changed when he was asked to stand by for a call from corporate headquarters in Philadelphia on Friday afternoon. He found out that he was scheduled for a conference with the CEO, John Giamacchi, the following week. He wondered what was up, but didn't worry about it. After checking into his hotel, he made the money delivery, which turned out to irritate the old man. It seems Max was a day late. Evidently, George Cravetz had always delivered the money promptly by five p.m. on the appointed Friday. Of course, Cravetz was a routine nut. Max came on Saturday instead of Friday, so what. The old geezer got his money. Max had hoped to get some information from this guy about George, but, apparently, the old man's days for giving out information were in the past. All he could remember is that the money came on time every month and had for years. He couldn't remember if Cravetz stayed in town or went back to Vegas right away. The only interesting thing he had to say is that he used to think he had a woman here. When Max asked what kind of woman, the old man just gave him a big wink.

"My brother said he thought George stayed with some woman when he came to town, but I don't think we ever looked into it." He stopped talking and seemed to go into some other world. Max wondered if he should leave.

"He's dead you know," the old man declared.

"George Cravetz?"

"My brother!" The old man was offended. "Who's George Cravetz?"

Max could see it was time to go. He was relieved to know that the old boy signed for the money. There was a receipt included in the moneybag and signing seemed part of the routine. At this point Max wasn't sure the man could even remember where the bathroom was, and he didn't want to be accused of not delivering the money because he couldn't remember that either. But now what? The trail to George Cravetz seemed to stop here. Max was certain that George was the key to this gold fiasco. He didn't know how much gold had been embezzled, but he knew however much it was, George was involved. Probably the sweaty guy, too. What was his name? Maybe there was a lead there. He was killed here in KC, that much he could remember. He just couldn't remember the name, but his secretary would know it. He wouldn't call her until Monday morning though. If she had to go into the office on Sunday, she might think something was up. He could wait until Monday.

Chapter 10

Las Vegas

Charlie Black had gotten into Vegas from the east coast on Friday night. He didn't go in to the casino until Saturday afternoon and he was surprised when Max wasn't in the building. Max always worked the casino on weekends. That's when the most action took place and he liked to be here for that. Charlie called down to the head cashier's office.

"Walter, who's on duty from the head office today?"

"Sam Burns. You want to see him?"

"Yes, see if you can find him. Send him up."

Five minutes later there was a knock on the door and Sam Burns came in.

"You want to see me, Mr. Black?"

"You're working for Max today?"

"All weekend. He said he had to be out of town for a few days. Wanted me to work. That's ok I hope?"

"Oh sure." Sam worked out of Max's office. It would be natural for Sam to fill in. It's just that he didn't know Max had out of town plans.

"I've been gone myself, Sam. I wanted to run some things by Max. You don't know where he went do you?"

"Sorry, no. All he told me was that he had to take care of some business for accounting."

"Accounting?"

"That's what he said."

"Ok, Sam. That's all I wanted. Thanks."

Sam Burns left and Charlie picked up the phone. He flipped through the employee directory and found Tom Woods' home number.

"Tom, it's Charlie Black."

"Oh, hey Mr. Black. Are you back in town?"

"Yes, I got back late last night. I was looking for Max, but they tell me he left town on some business for accounting."

"Yes, he's making the money delivery to KC since George hasn't come back. It was due this weekend."

"Oh, sure, that's great. Good to stay on schedule."

"That's right. We did everything just like George always does. Got Miss Alcott and security and counted out the money and filled out the ledgers. Mr. Grenwald even pulled out the gold and counted it."

Charlie stiffened. "He counted the gold?"

"Well, not all of it. He went through a few stacks, but said it was too time-consuming. He could just eyeball it and see that it was all there. George, of course, always counted the whole amount. But he could whip through the stacks really fast. All those years of practice, I guess."

"I guess. Thanks Tom. I can wait until Monday to talk to Max. Sorry to bother you at home."

"No problem. Anytime Mr. Black."

Charlie was not going to wait until Monday to talk to Max. He pulled up the airlines on line and booked a ticket on the red-eye to Kansas City. Then he called Max's secretary at home to find out where Max was staying. He said he needed to call him. She said he was booked at The Raphael, but reminded Charlie that Max had his cell phone with him.

"Oh, that's right! I'll try that number. Sorry I bothered you."

No calling. Face to face. But first… a trip to the vault.

He picked up a small scale from the table behind his secretary's desk that was used for office mail. Then went down to the vault room. The security guard was new to him, which suited him fine, and didn't question his request to open one of the safes. He quickly opened the gold safe, which he could do by himself because he *had* peeked when he and Miss Alcott returned the kilo bars that he had checked out. He began weighing the bars, placing them into two categories, real and fake. It was a lopsided score – 39 to 260.

Chapter 11

Kansas City

Charlie Black arrived in Kansas City shortly before six a.m. He didn't want to see Max right away, not out of consideration for the early hour, but because he had some business to attend to first. The flight was only three hours, but it gave him time to think through his present situation. Basically, the head office had shafted him. Not only did he not get a promotion now, it would be highly unlikely that he would get one in the foreseeable future. He would have to work for this new man, Phil Barcone, for a few years, *at least*, before he could expect a recommendation for advancement. He could quit and move back to the corporate world he had left, and he probably would. He had contacts that could introduce him back into that life. But first, maybe he should explore all of the possibilities here. The gold, for instance.

George took the gold. That much was certain. How Harry Crespi was involved was another matter, but he was involved. No other way to explain his murder in KC. Was he in on it with George and they had a falling out? Or had he tried to move in on George and get a share of the gold. That was much more likely. George Cravetz was not a man to have a partner. George must have killed him, and that was a shocking thought. From what he'd learned about the man, he would be hard pressed to step on a spider. How he came to have a nail gun, and *use* it, was the most troubling thought of all. He was cornered and dangerous.

The best thing to do would be to report all of this to the police. At this point why should he care what the casino management thought? He was moving on. Anyway, he could say he just discovered the missing gold and looked into it immediately. But... there was all of that gold out there somewhere. He wanted to do a little digging first. He would start with Max, just as soon as he got a gun. He wanted to arm himself in case he was stepping into a powder keg. He figured that George didn't have a gun, why use the nail gun, but Max might and he still wasn't sure what part Max was playing. He *had* checked the gold, after all.

Max had slept late on Sunday, usual for him because he always worked late nights at the casino and routinely slept in. He had a late breakfast at a restaurant nearby, walked around the shopping area looking in the windows, and bought a newspaper to take back to the hotel. He had just settled in with the sports section when there was a knock on the door. He opened it and there stood Charlie Black.

"Charlie, my god! What are you doing here?"

"I'm not sure, Max. Maybe just seeing what you're doing here."

"I delivered the money!" Max stood aside as Charlie walked into the room. "Yesterday... and the old boy said I was late!" Max was getting uncomfortable with the way Charlie was acting. "Said it was always delivered on Friday. But, what the hell, he got it didn't he."

"And you're still here? What are you doing still here? Visiting the museums, taking in the Opera? I'm surprised you're still here."

"What are you talking about? So what, I'm still here?"

"It just seems odd, Max. It's not that this isn't a great town, but a little slower than you usually like, that's all."

"Yeah, well what are you doing here? This isn't your usual kind of town either."

Both men stared at one another for a minute, and then Charlie said, "There's a problem at the casino and we need to talk."

"Yeah, I think there's a problem at the casino, too." Max wasn't quite sure how much to say. First, no telling what Black already knew, maybe he was the one lifting the gold, and if that was the case, it made him very dangerous.

Charlie had the same thought about Max. He didn't think Max was working with Cravetz, but maybe he was planning to push in on the scheme. The men were eyeing each other suspiciously.

"Tom Woods tells me you did an accounting of the gold in the vault," Charlie ventured.

"Yeah, he said it was part of the routine. Cravetz' routine. So that's what I did."

"What did you think?"

"About what? Look Charlie, if you've got something to say, spit it out. Quit beating around the bush."

"I checked out the gold, too. Last week."

"Woods told me."

"Well, what he doesn't know is that most of the gold in the vault is fake."

"God damn it! I knew there was something wrong!"

"Really? How did you know?"

"Because a guy comes into the casino making a stink about getting shafted in a payout. He says he took his winnings in gold, one of those kilo bars, and turns out it's fake! He even had an assay report to prove it."

"So, what did you do?"

"I calmed him down, and paid him cash. A lot of damn cash, too. Turns out that bar was worth more than fifty-seven thousand! I had to give him the exchange rate for the year he got the fake."

That worried Charlie. If word got out, no telling how many people would show up with fake bars claiming they got them at the casino. It's a blunder that could cost him his job, not that it mattered, but it would look bad on his record. Max wouldn't have to worry about that. His job was gone anyway. But there were other more dire consequences that could occur given the nature of the people they worked for. There were always rumors of the mob, certainly not individuals who would look kindly on the loss of millions of dollars.

"He didn't look like he was going to take this any further?"

"No, I practically made him a life time member of the Casino Perks Club. He seemed ok with that. I think he thought he'd have more of a fight to get his money. And here's the thing, maybe I should have given him a hard time. Who's to say that bar came from us? But I didn't want him dragging the cops into this."

"You've hit the nail on the head, Max. We don't want police or publicity." Charlie looked out of the window. The view was pleasant. The situation was not. "We've got a couple of problems here and the fallout could come down on both of us."

"What do you mean?" Max knew there was a problem. Gold was missing. What else?

Charlie was beginning to think Max probably didn't have anything to do with the gold switch, anymore than he did. But that wasn't going to mean much to the group they worked for.

Max was agitated. "What are you getting at Charlie? Why did you follow me here? You did follow me, didn't you?"

"Yes I did. I'm here because I'm looking for the gold."

"You think I stole the gold?" Max was outraged. "I think *you* stole the gold!"

"No, Max, I do not think you stole the gold, and I guess you'll just have to take my word for it that I didn't either. I'm pretty sure I do know who took it though." He hesitated a second and then added, "but I haven't ruled out the possibility that perhaps you were in on it."

"The hell you say! How do I know that you aren't in on it?" Max could feel his blood pressure rising.

"Good point, Max. You don't know. It looks like we are just going to have to trust each other for awhile."

Both men eyed each other. Charlie sat down in a chair by the window and nodded toward the bed. "Sit down Max. I've got a lot to tell you. In the first place there's about ten million dollars missing, depending on the day and the market price."

"Geeze! I had no idea that much was gone." Max felt the sweat break out on his upper lip. He hated sweating.

"And I think it was the bookkeeper, Cravetz, that took it."

"So do I! That's what I thought when I went through that *routine* business counting the gold. Why count every bar when they're stacked so you can see how many are there? He was doing a switch when he was messing with the stacks!"

"Exactly. It took him years to do it, but he made off with two hundred and sixty bars."

That brought a whistle from Max. "My god! So what are we going to do?"

"We're going to find Cravetz and the gold. So far, you and I seem to be the only ones who know about the switch, but I just found out that there's going to be a general audit in the near future. Maybe no one would notice the difference in the bars, but we can't take the chance."

"So. We just act like it's the first we know of it." Max shrugged his shoulders.

"Not going to work, Max. Too many people in accounting know that the two of us were checking the gold. Not to mention the security guard. We won't get away with pleading ignorance."

"Alright, we find the gold." He wrinkled his brow. "We look for Cravetz, right? Any ideas where to start?"

"A couple. What about the old man?"

Max snorted, "I asked the old guy when I was taking him the money about Cravetz and he said he thought he had a woman here."

"A woman! That's a new angle on Cravetz that I hadn't thought of." From all of the information that he had gathered on the man in Las Vegas, women were never part of the package. But who knew?

"Well, listen, the old boy couldn't remember we were even talking about Cravetz by the time I left, so maybe that's a dead end. But I got to thinking about that other individual from the Casino that was killed here, what's his name?"

"Harry Crespi."

"That's him! I couldn't remember his name, but I thought there might be a connection to Cravetz. It just seems odd that he was killed here in KC."

"I agree Max. I hope there's a connection here, because it's the only other lead I can see now. Who knows, maybe this is a dead end. Cravetz could have kept the gold in Las Vegas, but he's long gone from there. I checked his house a couple of days after he didn't come back to work and there was no sign of him. No car in the garage. Maybe he took off with the gold from there, and if that's the case, no telling where he went. So, I hope there's a lead here."

"This Crespi person, you think he was in on it with Cravetz?"

"No, I don't. Cravetz is a loner. It took him years to carry off all those bars and Harry Crespi wasn't a man of patience. I think Crespi tried to horn in on the gold. And..." he paused, "I think Cravetz killed him."

"That means he won't mind killing us if we find him." Max looked worried.

"I thought about that, but I don't think he has a gun and I do." Charlie patted his jacket pocket. "Crespi was killed with a nail gun, remember."

Max gave a slight shudder, "Well, I guess we should hope he doesn't have a chain saw." He paused. "He could be a long way away from here, you know. Then what?"

"At that point, I guess we quit." Charlie didn't say so to Max, but that *is* what he would do. He would quit Las Vegas before the loss was discovered because it could foul up his chances for a new job.

"So, what do we do?"

"Tomorrow morning we go see the police about Crespi. We'll just say we are in town on business and decided to see if they ever solved his murder. You know, a casino employee, so naturally we're interested."

"If we find Cravetz, what are we going to do with him?" Max worried. "Do we turn him in to the cops?"

Charlie thought for a minute. "We'll turn him in. Killing Crespi *and* ten million in gold makes him very dangerous."

Charlie had a plan. At this point, it did not include telling the police about George Cravetz. Max didn't need to know that. He wasn't sure what his plan for Max was, but he'd cross that bridge when he had to.

Chapter 12

Addie pounced on the phone when it rang. It was after ten but she was wide-awake. "Michael?"

"Yes. I'm not calling too late?"

Addie ignored that. "Michael, you are not going to believe this. It's worse then we thought!"

"What do you mean?"

"There are *fourteen* panels that open and they all have the same little compartments in them! Twelve of them are full, and the thirteenth one has eleven! Bars." She added that in case he didn't know what she was talking about. "One is empty."

"Good god!" Michael was dumbfounded. "How much is that?'

"Nine million, seven hundred and two thousand. I think." She had used the numbers that Michael used to calculate the worth of twenty bars. It sounded preposterous.

They were both silent for a minute and then Michael said, "Addie something bad is going on here."

"You're telling me! I haven't even thought about being scared up to now. But now I'm scared."

"Do you want me to come over?"

"Yes. No, you'd better not come over tonight. Rose and Helen will jump to conclusions."

"What conclusions?"

"Never mind. Just come over tomorrow. Better yet, come to the store. We get there a little before ten. It will seem natural for you to come to the store."

"Ok, I'll be there then." They hung up and Michael was left wondering what the conclusions could be.

Michael was in his car, waiting for them when Addie and Rose drove up to the store.

"Look, Addie, there's Michael! We're certainly seeing a lot of him these days." She cocked her head and gave her niece one of her inquiring looks. "Do you like him?"

Addie could feel her cheeks flushing. "Well, Rose, yes I do." No point acting coy. Rose would keep on until she had an admission out of her.

"That's nice. Helen and I like him, too." She said it as if the case was closed. They got out of the car and Michael joined them at the front door of the store.

"Good morning, Michael." Rose practically sang the greeting.

Addie hurried the lock and went in, waiting for someone to ask why her face was so red. Michael and Rose followed her.

"You're out early." Rose was continuing the song.

"Well, yes I am." He gave a pleading glance toward Addie.

"Michael and I have to go over some invoices." She knew that sounded lame.

"Oh, that's fine, just fine. Why don't you two take the books and go over to the bakery and have a cup of coffee and look into those invoices. I'll watch the store," she beamed.

Before Addie or Michael could react Rose clasped her hands together and said in a very distressed tone, "Oh no! I forgot! I have a dental appointment at 10:30! I'm going to have to leave in a few minutes, if I'm going to get there on time."

"Don't worry Rose. We can look at the books here. You go on to the dentist."

"Why don't I go get a couple of coffees and bring them back," Michael offered.

"Sure, that sounds great." Addie was relieved to get a little space between Rose and Michael. By the time he got back, Rose should be gone.

"Michael, I have to go to the police. This has really gotten out of hand." They were standing at the front counter of the store, nursing their coffee. "You will come with me, won't you?"

"Of course. Do you mean this morning?"

"I think so. Maybe when Rose gets back."

"You know this is going to cause a big stir, don't you? All of this money...gold... stashed in the walls of your house. The press is going to make a field day out of this."

"I thought about that. On the bright side, maybe it will be good free publicity for the store, if the store gets mentioned, that is."

"Yes, that's a point. What's the dark side?"

"Well, whose gold is it? I think it's pretty obvious that Mr. Barker stole it, don't you?"

"Yes, you don't make that kind of money selling plumbing fixtures."

"So now I think that Mr. Barker must have killed that person from Las Vegas! With the nail gun, no less!" She shook her head, "It just boggles my imagination to think of him doing a thing like that. He was such a mild mannered little man. He must have been desperate."

"'Desperate men do desperate things,'" Michael quoted.

"Good point. So the man from Las Vegas must have been trying to take the gold. The gun on the hallway floor that Helen picked up must have been his." She clapped her hands to her mouth. "Oh, my god! Mr. Barker killed him in our house!"

"Then stashed him in the gardener's truck? How did he do that without Helen finding out?"

"Helen goes out to the market most days at four. She walks and it usually takes about an hour before she's back home. It must have been then!" She brushed her hair distractedly from her face. "She said when she got home from the store she went up to ask Mr. Barker if he wanted to have dinner with us and she saw the gun lying on the floor outside his door. She picked it up, it went off and then she sees Mr. Barker flat on the floor in his room, and she thought she'd killed him." She paused, "The gun *must* have belonged to the other man. Surely it wasn't Mr. Barker's. He would have used that instead of the nail gun, wouldn't he?"

"You would think so. Where is the gun now?"

"I'm not sure. Rose or Helen must have put it away. The last time I remember thinking about that gun, it was on the table in the front hall."

"You never said anything about it to the police?"

"No. I never saw the connection. I don't know where I thought the gun came from. We were just glad that Helen hadn't shot Mr. Barker. We never mentioned it at the time, and then it seemed pointless. It really never occurred to me that the two things were related."

"But you knew Barker had a nail gun."

"You're right. I asked you what it was, but that's what it looked like from the first time I saw it. It's just that I couldn't imagine any scenario that included Mr. Barker being that aggressive!"

"He was pretty aggressive, alright." He paused, "You do know that someone else could be looking for the gold. Probably not the nicest person, either."

Addie nodded, "You're right. The sooner we get rid of it the better." She shook her head in wonderment. "This whole thing is just so bizarre!"

Chapter 13

Charlie Black presented himself at the Kansas City central police station very early Monday morning and asked to see someone about the man who was murdered a short time back. Charlie had said that Max could wait for him at the hotel, but Max waited in the rented car down the block from the station. He still wasn't sure he could trust Charlie. Maybe he really was in on it and was about to skip with the money. He would stay close to Charlie, very close.

Charlie was gone for quite awhile and it was beginning to make Max nervous. Maybe he went out the back door. Finally he came out.

"What took so long?"

"I had to wait for the detective in charge to get in. I told him I was in town on other business and just wanted to see if they had ever found out who killed Crespi."

"And?"

"They have no idea. They could never connect him to anyone in KC, and they never found the murder weapon. So it's been put on the back burner."

"So...that's a dead end for us."

"Maybe not. Harry's body was found at a recycle yard and they figured out it was a gardener's truck that dumped him. The gardener had no apparent connection to him so they checked out his stops that day, and found Harry's rental car on the same block where the gardener was working, but they couldn't find any connection to anyone in the neighborhood. They figured whoever was trying to get rid of Harry, happened to see the truck and dumped his body into it. He showed me a list of the places the gardener was working that day and asked if I knew anyone on it."

"And did you?"

"No, but there was an odd coincidence that happened on that day. An older man at the last stop died of a heart attack. The officer thought it was strange but never could connect the two."

"It could be our friend, Cravetz!"

"If it *is* him, and he's dead, then it means the gold is here. Maybe in that house."

"You know where this house is?"

"Yes, I've got the address right here." He tapped his head. "Let me put it into the GPS and then let's take a drive."

They found the house and circled the block before parking down the street.

"What do we do now?" Max leaned into the steering wheel and peered around.

Charlie was looking around, too, but there was no activity on the street. "I don't see anybody around, but someone might see us sitting here in the car and call the Neighborhood Watch or something, so let's just go knock on the door. No point to wait."

He opened the door and got out. Max followed and they walked down the street, up the front steps and crossed the porch. Charlie pushed the doorbell. They could hear it ringing but no one came to the door. Charlie tried it a few more times with the same result.

"Why don't we just go in and look around," Max suggested as he reached for his wallet. "I can pop this lock with a credit card easy."

"Relax. I'm not interested in being hauled in on a breaking and entering charge." He jabbed at the bell again and this time got results.

Helen had been in the basement doing the laundry when they first rang and she didn't hear the bell. She had come up the steps just in time to hear this last effort and went to the front door. She never opened the door to strangers when she was home alone, so she just peered through the sidelight and said, "Yes?"

Startled, Charlie looked around and saw her face in the window. "Good morning. I wonder if we could ask you a few questions about the gentleman who lived here?"

"Oh, my goodness. You police officers have asked so many questions! I can't imagine what else I can tell you."

Charlie glanced at Max then answered, "If we could just come in ma'am and look at his things again."

"Do you have some identification?"

Before Charlie could answer, Max flipped open his wallet, which was still in his hand, and flashed his employee ID card from the casino. "Yes, ma'am, right here."

Helen squinted through the glass and could see it was a picture ID. "Oh, well. I guess you can look again," she conceded as she opened the door.

The two men stepped into the front hall and looked around.

"We won't take long," Charlie reassured her. "If we could just take a look at his room..." It was a shot in the dark because Charlie wasn't sure what the living arrangements had been in this house. Maybe it was her room, too. He remembered what Max said about Cravetz having a "woman" in town. This one looked about Cravetz' speed. "And his personal things," he added.

"Oh, poor Mr. Barker didn't have many personal things," said Helen shaking her head sadly.

"Who's Mr. Barker?" blurted Max. "We're looking for George Cravetz."

"George Cravetz? I have no idea who that is. I thought you were talking about Mr. Barker." Helen was worried now that she shouldn't have opened the door. "I think you have the wrong house."

Charlie was annoyed that Max had opened his mouth. "Maybe we're talking about the same person," he hastened to say, as she seemed about to open the front door. "The individual we're looking for is about sixty, gray hair, maybe five foot seven or eight."

"Well...yes, that's just what Mr. Barker looked like, but his name wasn't Cravetz and he's dead now, so you're not going to find him here," she said with finality.

"If we could just look at his personal things," Charlie said again.

Helen didn't like this. She was beginning to think that these men were not police officers, and, if not, who were they? "Maybe you could come back later." She edged toward the front door.

"Well, we don't want to put you out," Charlie said smoothly, "but why don't we just take a look now as long as we're here."

Helen could see that they weren't going to leave without looking into Mr. Barker's things. She was positive now that they weren't police.

"Well, yes then. Let me just show you where they are." She led them toward the open door to the basement. The light was still on and she started down.

"They're down there?" Max asked.

"Oh, yes. We put everything in the storage locker after the funeral."

They clattered down the wooden stairway into a rather large basement. It was typical of the kind in these old houses. The walls were made of natural stone, and the floor of cement. It smelled of bleach and bluing, and housed the kind of old furniture relegated to attics and basements. There was a large furnace, a relatively modern washer and dryer next to the old wringer washing machine, and a clothesline strung up nearby. The light came from two light bulbs, one at each end of the room, screwed into fixtures in the ceiling. Along one wall there were individual lockers used for storage. They had wooden walls to separate them and doors consisting of metal bars, which could be locked with padlocks, although none were. All in all it looked remarkably like a jail. One of them had been used for coal storage in the days when that was their heating fuel, but now it held shovels and garden tools. Winter coats were hanging in another. Helen stopped in front of a third locker that contained several trunks and a number of suitcases.

"His things are in here," she said, holding the door open, "up on that top shelf. You'll have to get them down yourselves. It's too high for me."

Max and Charlie looked at the assortment of bags and Max stepped into the locker.

"All those bags up there?" asked Max.

"Oh, I don't think they are all his. You'll just have to look. We didn't know what to do with his things after he died, poor man, no friends or family that we could find. Everything is there."

"Give me a hand Charlie." Max had started to pull down a rather large suitcase and Charlie stepped in to help him hand it down.

Helen quietly closed the door, took the open padlock out of the hasp, closed the latch, reinserted the lock, snapped it shut, and removed the key. It was the click of the lock that caught the men's attention.

"Hey, lady! What are you doing?" Max still held the suitcase over his head.

Charlie rattled the door, but it didn't give. "Wait a minute!" he called to Helen's retreating figure. "Where are you going?"

"You're not police officers," Helen called down from the safety of the upstairs doorway. "I don't know who you are, but you're not police officers!"

"Ma'am, come back! We can explain!" Charlie did not want her calling the police. No publicity! "Please! Let us explain!"

By this time Helen had reached the phone in the hall and was dialing the number for the store.

Rose had just returned from the dentist and found Addie helping a customer.

"Michael left?" Rose sounded very disappointed

"He's coming back soon." He had gone to take care of another account not far away, but would be back in time to go with Addie to the police station.

Rose looked at the clock on the counter. "You should go to lunch with him."

"Yes, well maybe I will." Addie still didn't want to say anything about going to the police to Rose here in the store. It was too much to explain, especially if customers were around. She still hadn't worked out how she was going to explain it to the police.

The phone rang just as Michael walked through the door.

"You two run on to lunch," said Rose, reaching for the phone. "I'll take care of the store. 'Good morning. The Vintage House,'" she used her singing voice again. "Oh, Helen, what do you want dear?" She was shooing Addie and Michael toward the door, but then stopped. "You did what?"

The alarm in Rose's voice caused Addie to turn back. "What's wrong?"

Rose clasped the phone to her chest and said in a lowered voice, "She says she's captured two men in the basement!"

Addie stared at Rose for a minute, and then said, "Give me the phone." Rose handed it over. "Helen? What's the matter?"

"Oh, I thought those two men were the police!" Helen said in a rush. "They said they wanted to see Mr. Barker's room and his things, so I let them in, but they started calling him by another name, and then I couldn't get them to leave so I locked them in the luggage locker in the basement." She paused, but when Addie didn't answer she added. "I think you should come home."

"Yes, alright. I'll be right there. Where are you now?"

"In the front hall."

"You're sure they're locked up?" Addie wasn't sure why this conversation didn't surprise her.

"Oh yes. They can't get away," Helen said with remarkable assurance. "I took the key out of the padlock."

"Good thinking. But wait for me on the front porch, just to be safe. I'll be home in ten minutes." She hung up and looked at Rose and Michael. "It's an emergency. I have to go."

"Addie!" Rose was agitated. "What's the matter with Helen? Why is she saying these things?"

"What's wrong?" Michael was alarmed. Both women looked like they were on the verge of hysteria. "Has something happened to Aunt Helen?"

"Yes. Well, yes and no," Addie glanced around the store but there were no shoppers at the moment, a mixed blessing. "It seems that two men showed up at the house wanting to see Mr. Barker's things, and Helen got suspicious and locked them in the basement." She stopped. "That's an abridged version," she finished.

They all observed a moment of silence, 'in deference to the world tilting out of plumb,' thought Addie.

Rose began to dither, "I was afraid this was going to happen!"

"You were?" Addie was amazed.

"She's going round the bend. First that gun business. I don't believe she even shot that gun! I think she made up that whole story. And now this! Really! She captured two men?" Rose paused to take a huffy breath. "I've *never* known her to act like this! She's just losing it, and, if that's not the case, then she's being very, very silly." Her voice trailed off, "Oh, I'm so worried about her."

A fleeting doubt crossed Addie's mind. They never had found a bullet hole anywhere. "Well, let's hope for the best," Addie had calmed down. "I'll run home and see what this is all about."

"I'm coming with you!" Rose was adamant. She was already fishing around in the drawer behind the counter and came up with a small sign, neatly printed: 'Sorry – Gone to Lunch – Please Come Back.' There were two small clock faces under the message, one to indicate when they left and the other to say when they would be back. Rose put it in the front window.

Michael had watched all of this without saying anything, but he was worried. There could be more to this than either woman realized.

"I'll go with you." It wasn't an offer so much as a statement. "My car's right out front."

Chapter 14

Charlie and Max had heard the woman make a phone call and then a door opened and closed.

"What the hell?" Max exploded. "What's she doing?"

"She called the police, would be my guess," Charlie rattled the door again and then began looking at the hinges. He'd need some kind of tool if he was going to be able to pry them apart.

"Holy crap." Max looked very worried. "They can't get us for anything, can they? She let us in...so we weren't breaking and entering."

"The truth is, Max, we might not be able to prove that." He had started looking into some of the suitcases to see if he could find any kind of tool, or file, something to lever the hinges off of the wooden frame. "In fact, she let us in because she thought we were the police, so we might be facing an 'impersonating police' charge."

"We never said we were cops!"

"Well, maybe not, but we sure led her to believe it." By this time Charlie had abandoned the search. He rattled the door once more then sat down on one of the trunks.

"So, what are we going to say?" Max had begun cracking his knuckles, profoundly annoying Charlie.

"Can you stop that?"

Max looked down at his hands and then jammed them in his pockets. "Sorry."

"We've got two problems," Charlie ran his fingers through his hair. "The first one is how not to get arrested. Maybe we use the fact that there was a name mix-up. We said one name and she said another and then we explain to the police that we asked to see his things to see if it *was* Cravetz." He thought about that for a minute. "That might be believable. We just say that this was a person that disappeared from work and we were looking for him. We were worried."

"That's good," declared Max. "And the old lady got some crazy idea we were the police and freaked out." He hesitated. "What's the other problem?"

"The gold. This dead guy was Cravetz, I'm sure of that. The detective told me that it was an odd coincidence that this guy dies the same day that Crespi is killed. But I think Cravetz killed him"

"And then drops dead?" Max was trying to follow Charlie's thinking.

"I know, it doesn't seem likely, but I think that's just what happened. And the detective also said that this person that dropped dead had been a renter in this house for years," he looked at Max. "Years. That means he's had years to stash the gold."

"What? You think it's here in this house?"

"I hope so, but it could be in a bank. He was an accountant, so he might have kept it at a bank in a safety deposit box, but somehow I don't think so. And, if it's in a bank we won't get it back without the story hitting the papers."

"So, maybe it's here. We didn't look in all of the suitcases," he was eyeing the luggage on the top shelf.

"It's not up there. A kilo bar weighs about two pounds, which means there's five hundred pounds of gold missing. It's not in any suitcase on a top shelf."

"What about these trunks? It could be in them!" Max opened the one Charlie wasn't sitting on and found it empty. Charlie stood up and pushed against the other trunk. It moved easily.

"Not in here. I wouldn't be able to budge it if it was." He sat down again.

Max sat down on the other trunk. "So what do we do?"

"We wait. We deal with the police first, and then the gold."

Helen was waiting on the front porch when Michael drove into the driveway with the two women. Addie was out of the car first and up the steps.

"Helen, what's going on?" Rose and Michael were right behind her.

"I know I shouldn't have let those men into the house," Helen said apologetically, "but I thought they were policemen."

"What made you think that?"

"I asked if they had any identification and one of them showed me his."

"Was it a badge?" asked Michael.

"No...I don't remember a badge, just a picture ID. I looked at it through the window before I opened the door."

"Helen! You could have been murdered!" Rose was beside herself.

"Oh Rose, don't scold me." Helen was on the verge of tears. "I didn't have any idea that this would happen!"

Addie jumped in before both women began crying. "Do you really have them locked up in the basement?" The idea seemed preposterous.

"Oh yes. They're locked up."

"How did you manage that?" Michael was trying to envision this 'capture' event with no luck.

"Oh, well, it wasn't very hard." Helen had regained her composure and now seemed rather matter-of-fact about the whole thing. "When I saw that they weren't going to leave without seeing Mr. Barker's things, I said I would show them. I took them down to the basement to the luggage locker. They went in and I locked the door." She stopped talking and looked at the three people staring at her. "Then I called you," she said.

"And I went out on the porch to wait for you," she added when no one spoke.

"Wow, Helen!" Michael was the first to break the silence. "That was pretty gutsy of you."

"What makes you think they aren't police officers?" Addie asked. Maybe they really were police officers and Helen just locked them up.

"Oh no! They aren't police officers! I knew that the minute they called Mr. Barker by another name...Dick Cavett, or some such. Real police officers wouldn't to that." Helen had assumed a righteous stance by now.

"Did they have guns?" Rose wanted to know.

"Well, they weren't holding any guns that I could see. They could have had them in their pockets, I suppose."

"Ladies," Michael broke in, "we better get on with this. We need to find out what's going on."

"Do you think we should call the police now?" asked Addie. Her trip to the police station had been on her mind all day, and this was just proving that she should have gone sooner.

"Let me just check on these guys before we do that." Michael wanted to have a little more information about who was captive in the basement before he made the call...if there were captives. After all, he didn't know Addie's aunts well enough to know if this might just be in Helen's imagination. On the other hand, maybe that bad feeling that he had at the store could have some validity, considering the gold in the upstairs bedroom. Maybe these men, if there really were two men, were after the gold, which would make them very dangerous.

He cautiously opened the front door and went in.

"Michael, be careful!" Addie warned.

"Oh Michael, do you want a gun?" Rose asked. "We have a gun if you need one."

"Helen, you're sure they're locked up?" he asked. The thought of guns began to make him nervous.

"Yes, here's the key," and she produced it from her apron pocket.

"It won't take me a minute to get," declared Rose. "It's right here in the top drawer of the buffet." All three women had followed him into the front hall and Rose was heading into the dinning room. "I'm sure it has bullets in it. It's the gun that Helen used when she thought she'd killed Mr. Barker."

"Oh Rose, don't bring that up again!" Helen was exasperated.

"No, that's ok," said Michael. "If it looks like I need a gun, we'll call the police right away. I'm just going to take a look at them. I won't go all the way down." He was still leaning toward disbelief about this whole thing anyway.

"Be careful!" Addie repeated.

Both Charlie and Max stood up when they heard a door open upstairs. They could hear people talking, but couldn't catch what they said. The next thing they knew there was a man coming down the first few basement steps. He bent down and peered at them from a safe distance.

"Well, I'll be damned," said Michael under his breath. "She did catch two men."

There was a moment of silence and then Charlie said, "We can explain...are you police?"

"No," answered Michael, "but they can be here in a hurry."

"Wait! Give us a chance to explain."

Max chimed in. "We didn't mean any harm... it was just a misunderstanding."

"Who are you?" Michael asked.

Charlie and Max looked at each other for a moment, and then Charlie said, "We work at a casino in Las Vegas." He stopped. That didn't sound too good. "Look, we were in town on other business and as long as we were here we thought we would see if we could track down one of the employees at our work that's been missing for awhile." Charlie stopped, but when Michael didn't say anything, he went on. "This person made regular trips to KC for years and then he just disappeared."

"What's his name?"

"George Cravetz. The lady upstairs didn't recognize the name, but when we described him she thought it might be the same person."

"Yeah, she said we could look at his personal things, and then she locks us in here!" Max sounded aggrieved.

"Just a minute," said Michael and he went back upstairs.

Max and Charlie sat back down. "You think he's calling the cops?" Max was worried.

"Maybe. We just have to sit here and wait."

"Use your cell phone! *We* should call the police! That old woman locked us up unlawfully."

"Max." Charlie lowered his voice. "Use your head. We don't want the police here. It'll make finding the gold very difficult. Relax. Just wait." The last thing Charlie wanted was the police butting in. Now that he knew Gorge Cravetz was dead it meant that only two people knew the gold was missing – he and Max. This was becoming more promising by the minute, but it all depended on how things went with these people.

Michael returned to the women who were hovering in the hall. Rose had retrieved the gun, which she offered to Michael.

"Thanks, Rose," he said taking the gun. "I hope we won't need this." He ran his hand through his hair. "Listen, we have to talk. I'm not sure what's going on here. These men want a chance to explain, and I'm inclined to listen to them before we call the police. They say that they're looking for someone who sounds like your Mr. Barker, that he's missing from work."

"Why did they look here?" asked Addie. "What made them think he was Mr. Barker?"

"That I don't know." He looked at the three women. "What do you think, do we listen?"

"We can listen," said Addie, "from a distance. Don't unlock them."

"How do we know who they are?" asked Rose. "They can say anything."

"Good point, Rose," said Michael. "We'll see about that first." He turned back toward the basement door. Again he only went as far as the first few steps.

"Can you prove who you are?" he called to the men. They were peering through the bars at Michael's dim figure at the top of the stairs.

"I've got a way you can check, if you've got Internet access," said Charlie, thinking it was a lot to assume they had a computer, let alone Internet access.

"What are we checking?"

"If you can get on the Casino website, I can give you an admin password. You can look us up. There's an employee directory and it includes pictures."

Michael turned back to the women. "Did you hear that? Addie do you have a computer?"

"Yes. And the Internet." Getting connected to the Internet had been one of the first things she had done when she moved back from Chicago. It helped. "My computer is in my room. I'll get it." She was back in a few minutes with a laptop that she opened up on the dining room table and clicked to life. "What are we looking up?"

"Ok," Michael called back down, "give us the website."

Charlie gave them the website address and included the admin password, which Addie typed in. Sure enough, the casino employee page came up. "Here it is," she said.

Michael looked at it over her shoulder. "There's a link to the employee directory. Click on that." The page opened up.

"Ok, we've got it," Michael called down. "What are your names?"

"Charles Black and Max Grenwald."

Michael repeated the names to Addie.

"Employees are listed under departments," she looked at Michael. "I'll try management?"

"Sure."

"Oh look, here's Charles Black. It says he's assistant to the manager." She put in Max Grenwald. "Well, look at this...he's the manager." She looked up at the three who were hovering around her.

"Are there any pictures?" asked Rose.

"Yes. Helen look here," directed Addie. "Are these the men in the basement?"

Helen leaned in closer to the computer and nodded her head. "I think so." She didn't sound positive.

"Do *you* think they look like their pictures?" Rose asked Michael.

"I can't say for sure. I'll have to get closer to them." He glanced at the gun that he had put down on the dining room table, but picked up the computer instead. As he headed for the basement all three women cautioned, in unison, "Be careful!"

"Oh, what if they have guns!" Helen's experience with a gun had left its mark. "You should take this gun!"

"Now, don't worry. I don't want this to turn into a shoot-out," he smiled. But he could see their very real alarm. "Really, don't worry. They won't try anything. They're locked up. They know we can call the police."

"Well, I'm going to stand right by the phone!" declared Rose.

Michael carried the open computer down to the bottom of the stairs. "I need to see you a little better." Both men stood at the locked door as Michael clicked back and forth from one picture to the next. It was them.

"Why don't you look up George Cravetz, while you're at it," said Charlie.

"Ok. What department?"

"Accounting."

He brought up the picture of a small gray-haired man. "Ok, I've got him. Let me show this to the ladies and see if they recognize him."

"You're gonna see we're telling the truth!" Max declared. "The lady shouldn't have locked us up!" His anxiousness was being replaced with righteous indignation.

"Take it easy, Max," said Charlie. Things were working out. No point to irritate the folks.

Michael had gone back upstairs with the picture of George Cravetz up on the computer screen.

"Take a look at this person. Is this your Mr. Barker?" He turned the computer so that they all had a good view.

"Oh, my lands!" Helen clapped her hands to her face. "Rose, look! It's Mr. Barker!"

For once, Rose seemed speechless. She stared at the picture, wrinkled her brow, and finally said, "Well, I'll be. I'll just be!"

"That's him," confirmed Addie. She looked at Michael. "Should we let them out?"

He shook his head. "Not yet. We have to think about this." He hesitated. "We have to talk about upstairs," he said to Addie. "I think maybe your aunts need to know about upstairs."

"Upstairs? What's upstairs?" asked Rose.

"Do you think all of that...stuff came from the casino?" Addie looked toward the upstairs as she said that.

"Stuff? What stuff?" Rose was becoming agitated. "What are the two of you talking about?"

"I do," said Michael. "I think we should take a minute before we turn these men loose. We should all be on the same page. I don't think there could be any problem for the three of you with this, but I just want to talk it out first."

"You're right," Addie agreed. "Rose, Helen we have something we have to show you."

By this time the alarm on the older ladies faces was palpable.

"You haven't found a dead body, have you?" Helen whispered.

"No. No dead bodies," Addie reassured her. "Something else quite different. Let's go upstairs."

"Wait a minute," said Michael as he went back once more to the basement doorway and called down to the men. "We'll be back with you soon."

"What do you mean?" cried Max. "Where are you going?" When he got no answer he called out, "Hey, come back! Charlie, do something!"

"I am, Max," said Charlie. "I'm waiting."

Addie led the way upstairs with Michael bringing up the rear. In between Helen and Rose had begun to cling to one another. In the realm of 'alarming days,' this one threatened to surpass the day that Mr. Barker died. They all trooped into the sunlit bedroom and stood looking at one another.

"Well?" said Rose.

"I'm not sure where to start," Addie confessed. "There is so much about Mr. Barker that's hard to believe." She looked out of the window into the peacefulness of the shaded backyard. It was hard to imagine all of the skullduggery that had happened here, in this very room. She turned back to her aunts.

"First, Mr. Barker... Cravetz. Cravetz?" She looked at Michael.

He nodded. "Cravetz." He flipped open the computer which he had carried upstairs and clicked on the picture of George Cravetz. "Here he is...in the accounting department." He turned the computer towards the women. "In fact, head of accounting."

Helen and Rose peered at the picture and the little bit of biographical information next to it.

"It says he worked there for forty years!" Rose was flabbergasted. "How can that be?"

"You don't suppose that's Mr. Barker's twin, do you?" Helen asked hopefully.

"No, I'm afraid not." Addie felt sorry for her aunts. This man, who had become an accepted part of life around this house, was turning out to be sort of a modern day Jekyll and Hyde. "There are some things about Mr. Barker that you need to know...before we let those men out of the basement. I want you to hear all of this from Michael and me."

"Addie!" Rose was alarmed. "What in the world are you talking about?"

"I'm not sure where to begin." There was so much to tell. "Well...at least now we know why Mr. Barker never talked about himself, or anything else. He had a secret life here...well, really he had a secret life in Las Vegas." She turned to Michael. "Where do I start?"

"I think we should show them what we found, and go from there." He picked up the carpentry case and set it on the table. "Addie asked me to take a look at this toolbox the other day because she wondered what this tool was." He lifted the nail gun out of the case...and I told her it was a nail gun." Rose and Helen looked at him quizzically, but said nothing, so he went on. "The other thing I saw in here was this piece of hardware." He picked up the pressure latch and showed it to them.

"What is it?" asked Rose.

"It's a magnetic latch that's used for cabinets or doors when there's no doorknob. You push on it and the door opens. It seemed out of place here. Mr. Barker was installing panels, not cabinets, so Addie and I started looking for a cabinet." He knelt down next to the wall and pushed on the bottom corner of the panel in front of him. "This is what we found." The door swung open to reveal the treasure.

"Oh my!" exclaimed Helen. "Look at that!"

"What is that?" asked Rose, peering at the bewildering contents. "Is it insulation?"

"That's what I thought," said Addie smiling ruefully. "No, it's gold, and it's worth a lot of money."

"Where did it come from?"

"Mr. Barker was stealing it from the casino. It's the only explanation."

"Oh, that just can't be!" Helen looked close to tears.

"I think it has to be," said Addie softly. "These men in the basement came looking for him...Cravetz...because he has been missing from work."

"Oh yes," agreed Rose. "He couldn't go back to work because he died. And you think he took all of this?" She gestured toward the gold.

"Yes," said Michael, "and a lot more." He began going from panel to panel pushing on the latches until they all swung open.

"All this time, we thought he was such a sweet man." Helen said. "I was always so worried that he spent too much time alone, and all along he was hiding all of this."

"He wasn't finished, was he?" Rose was looking at the few empty panels. "If he hadn't died he would still be doing this, wouldn't he?"

"Well, I'm not sure," Addie regretted having to tell her aunts the rest of the bad news about Mr. Barker. A thief was one thing, but a murderer...that was another level altogether. "There's more, I'm afraid. Do you remember the police asking about the murdered man they found in the landfill? They said he'd been dumped there by our gardener?"

"Yes," answered Rose. "What about him?"

Addie looked at Michael, took a deep breath, and plunged ahead. "Michael and I think Mr. Barker killed him."

"What!" Rose was working her way up to hysteria.

"Oh, that can't be!" Helen was dissolving into tears. "That man was a thug! Why would Mr. Barker be involved with a thug?"

"I think that man, the thug, must have been threatening Mr. Barker," said Michael. "Barker was cornered and he killed him."

"With the gun I found?" asked Helen.

"I'm afraid not, Helen." Addie shook her head. "That gun must have belonged to the murdered man. Maybe he was threatening Mr. Barker with it." She paused. "Remember what the police told us? The man was killed with a nail gun."

The implications of this statement dawned on the women. They looked stunned. "Oh that's too horrible!" Rose was distraught. "Are you telling us Mr. Barker killed that man with a nail gun?"

Addie nodded and then put her arms around both of the women and pulled them close to her. This was an awful shock. These two good women were out of their depth with this gruesome revelation about a man they thought they knew so well. They had mourned his death once and now it was as if he had just died again. When their tears subsided, Addie said, "We wanted you to know this before we talk to those men downstairs."

Chapter 15

Charlie and Max were left sitting on the trunks when Michael and the women went upstairs. Max was still fuming about being locked up, but Charlie was more optimistic. It looked like the police weren't going to be called, at least not yet, and the prospect of finding the gold was looking better. Ever since Charlie had been given the news about the coming new management and his resulting stagnant position with the casino, he had fantasized about the gold. Now that he was sitting here in this house, with the gold within reach, at least he hoped so, his fantasy had taken a sharp turn toward reality. He still didn't know how this would play out. He would have to see what came of this present fiasco, but he had always been good at judging situations and making the most of them when the stakes were high, and a multi-million dollar stake was worth the effort. As far as he could see, the main impediment to his plan was Max. Max was not an innovative thinker, which was why he was losing his job. But Charlie had worked with him long enough to know that Max listened to him when it came to business matters. He also knew that Max had no personal connections in Las Vegas. Like himself, Max had been married, maybe even several times, but wasn't now. Charlie decided to take a chance. Worst-case scenario, Max could tell him he was out of his mind, and maybe he was.

"Max, I've got a feeling that we're going to find the gold."

"Yeah? What gives you that feeling? The only feeling I'm getting is we're in some kind of a nut house." He stood up and began shaking the locked door again as if, at last, it would open. "What are these people up to? Do you think they're calling the cops?"

Charlie shrugged. "They could be, but somehow I don't think so. It's been long enough for someone to show up, and no one has." Charlie paused and regarded Max again. If he was going to go through with this, he had to say something now.

"Max, I've got an idea about the gold that I want to discuss."

"Yeah? What?" Max rubbed his hands over his face and then stared at Charlie.

"First, I have to fill you in on a little company business."

"Company?"

"Casino. When I left Vegas the other day I went back to the head office. Frank called and said I should come back there for my performance review. I thought that it meant I was getting a promotion because every other time the review happened in Vegas."

"Yeah, I'm going back this week. Head office called me, too."

"I know. They told me. So, here's the kicker. I got a good review, and I'm going to make a little more money, but there was no promotion and it doesn't look like there's going to be one anytime soon."

"Sorry to hear that." Max wondered why Charlie was telling him this. "So they called you all the way back there to tell you that?"

"No, that wasn't the only reason. They wanted to introduce me to my new boss, Phil Barcone."

Max knew Phil. They attended management meetings together. He knew that Phil managed the Atlantic City casino. "They're moving you to Jersey?"

"No, I'm not moving to Jersey." Charlie gave Max a long look. "I'm staying right where I am. They're closing Atlantic City and moving Barcone to Vegas."

Max said nothing, but Charlie could feel the turmoil boiling up inside of him. Finally he exploded, "My job! He's taking my job."

Charlie nodded, "That's why they're bringing you back east. They're going to tell you there."

Max turned his back on Charlie and gripped the bars of the door. He was so outraged that he felt as if he could bend the bars with his bare hands. All of these years! He'd worked his ass off to get where he was, working his way up, from picking up cigarette butts off the casino floor, to supervising busboys, to breaking into management, and finally getting to the top. What? He was out?

He whirled around and demanded, "Who told you?"

"John Giamacchi."

Max didn't know what to say. It must be true. Why would Charlie tell him this and then have to go back to work with him. Max dropped back down on the trunk and put his head in his hands. "Christ, Charlie." He looked up. "Where does that leave me? I don't want to start all over." He shook his head and looked down at his hands, maybe hoping the answers would pop up on his palms.

"I have an idea Max. It's pretty radical." He stopped and waited for Max to respond.

"What?"

"You see, the two of us are in the same boat, so to speak. The Casino is pushing on both of us – me into a corner, and you, basically off the roof."

Max said nothing but he was listening.

"As far as I'm concerned," Charlie went on, "I'm through in Vegas. I don't want to wait around on the off chance that I might move up. I can go back to the corporate life I left."

"Great for you. I don't have a place to go back to."

"Well, I don't really want to go back to that other life either, if I don't have to...and I think I have a way out...for both of us, if you're interested."

Sometimes Max gave the appearance of being a little slow on the uptake, but it would be a mistake to believe that. His ability to read the situation confronting him had gotten him where he was now. He knew what Charlie was driving at.

"The gold."

Charlie nodded, "That's right. The gold."

Max was quiet for a minute. He had never had a larcenous heart, but then he'd never been faced with corporate treachery and the prospect of humiliation. It *would* be humiliating to get sacked.

"I'm interested." Max amazed himself at how easy it was to go over to the dark side, or maybe it was the bright side. "Do you have a plan?"

"I think I do."

"You *think* you do? I'm not interested in spending the rest of my life behind bars." He looked around at his surroundings. "This is enough for me."

"Well, the plan depends on what happens next." Charlie glanced toward the upstairs. "We need to find the gold, of course, but the fact that Cravetz *and* Crespi are dead means that you and I are the only two who know the gold is missing from the casino."

"What about this group?" Max hoped Charlie didn't have murder in mind. He wasn't up for that, but he remembered Charlie had a gun. "They'll know, won't they?"

"I don't know. Probably. That is, if the gold's here. That's why we have to see what happens next."

"Let's say it is, and let's say we figure out how to deal with these people...how are we getting away with the gold?"

"My first thought was to just take it and leave the country, but that's not practical...on a lot of levels. First, we'd never get it over the border. Second, if both of us fail to return to Vegas, and soon, there'll be a manhunt out for us, and it won't be the cops. The organization will figure out something is going on and they'll question everybody in Vegas, and like I said, the accounting department *and* security know that both of us were checking the gold. They'll figure out what happened and they'll find us. I have every confidence in their ability to find us." Max said nothing so Charlie went on. "If the gold is here, we have to drive it back to Vegas."

"Vegas?" Max was confused.

"Well, maybe I should have said *toward* Vegas. We drive toward Vegas and we put it into self-storage facilities along the way."

"Self-storage? Why not a bank...in safety deposit boxes?"

"I thought about that. The gold's too heavy and we'd each have a hundred and thirty bars to park. That's two hundred and sixty pounds." Charlie had been giving this serious thought and was becoming a firm believer in his own plan. "If you even put twenty bars in one box it would weigh forty pounds. Usually banks bring out your box and put it on a table for you to open in privacy, and they'd wonder about the weight. And, at the rate of twenty or so bars in a box, you'd need six boxes, six different banks." Charlie shook his head. "That would take days to open the accounts. We don't have the time."

"Ok, I get it. So we use public storage."

"We each have our own storage locker, probably not even in the same facility. Then no one sees us together and we come back whenever it suits us and pick it up. We'll each be on our own."

"How many bars did you say?"

"Two hundred sixty are missing, so we each get one hundred and thirty." He paused, and then added, "That's a little over five million each if you figure the market price right now."

Max closed his eyes and let out a deep breath. This was a bigger retirement package than he had ever thought he would get. He could live just fine on this. He opened his eyes and looked at Charlie. "You can't do this unless I'm in on it, can you."

"No. I can't. Not that I wouldn't rather have it all, but I'd have to trust that you wouldn't tell anyone...or else..."

"You'd have to get rid of me," Max finished.

That amused Charlie. "I hadn't gone quite that far," he observed, "but I did think I would have to give up the idea if you wouldn't get on board. If we do this, we both need to fade from the scene as soon as it can be managed. Eventually, the fake gold will be discovered and there will be hell to pay. We should be a long way off when that happens." Max listened. "You can move on right away. They'll give you a retirement party and some kind of a pay-off and you can retire to Tahiti, or some such, with no questions asked."

"What about you? What's your plan?"

"I'll have to stay for awhile and work with Phil Barcone. That actually works to our advantage when it comes time to do the audit. I don't think anyone will suspect that the gold is fake at a glance, and I think I can keep the inspection to a sight count."

"Yeah," Max agreed, "It's pointless to count the individual bars when they're stacked so neatly."

"It could be years before it's discovered."

"Unless you get another unhappy customer with a plug bar," Max reminded him.

"You're right. Well, I'm not planning to stay long. I'll get a job offer back east and be on my way."

Both men were quiet for a few minutes.

"Well?" asked Charlie. "Are you in?"

"I'm in," said Max, just in time, because they could hear the voices upstairs coming closer to the basement door.

"So, let's see how this plays out." Charlie looked expectantly toward the stairs.

Addie and Michael had decided that they would listen to what the men had to say. After all, their identities proved valid according to the website information. Helen and Rose agreed, but would probably have agreed to anything considering the state that all of this had brought them to. They were vacillating from shock to indignation to just plain bewilderment about all that they had just learned about their Mr. Barker.

"What do you think," Addie asked. "Do we let them out?"

"I think I'd rather hear what they have to say first," Michael answered. "We can go downstairs and listen."

That galvanized Rose out of the doldrums. "They could have guns! What if they shoot us?"

"Rose, they won't shoot us," Michael said calmly. "You ladies stay at the top of the stairs and they'll know that you will call the police if they try anything."

"Rose, you and Helen stay up here. I'm going down with Michael. Don't argue," she added as she could see that her aunts were about to protest. "Michael's right. They aren't going to shoot us from inside a locked cage."

Michael was already starting down the stairs and Addie followed him. The two men had stood up and were waiting.

"Ok," said Michael. "We'll listen to what you have to say."

"You could see we are who we say we are, am I right?" asked Charlie. Michael nodded. "So, is the man, George Cravetz, the man who lived here?"

"Yes," Addie spoke up. "It was a shock to see him there on the website, but it was Mr. Barker."

"I'm just going to guess the next part, but I think I'm right. He came here to this house once a month for many years just for a weekend and then he spent a week here each summer." He could see that he was right just looking at the reaction on Addie's face.

"How did you know that?" she asked.

"Because it was part of his job to make a trip to Kansas City each month to deliver a payment to persons here. And one week out of the year he went on vacation. By himself," he added. "The people in his office thought he went camping in the desert because that's what he said...*and* he brought back drawings of the desert."

"The sketch book in his room!" Addie realized that this was what Mr. Barker was doing. Sketching from the birding book, or whatever it was.

"Max and I are pretty sure we know what he was doing all these years, besides casino business...how many years was he here?"

"More than twenty," said Addie. "I'd have to ask my aunts the exact number."

"Well, that gave him plenty of time," offered Max.

"Time for what?" asked Michael. He wanted to hear them give a reason before he and Addie offered too much information.

"A large amount of gold has disappeared from the vault at the casino," said Charlie, "and it had to be Cravetz that took it. It would have taken him years to switch out the real kilo bars for fakes, but that's what happened."

Addie and Michael looked at each other. Then Michael said, "You're here looking for that gold?"

"Yes. We were looking for Cravetz, too, but now that he's dead, we're just looking for the gold."

"Why look here?"

"It was a hunch, really," admitted Charlie. "We checked with the police about the murder of one of our other employees, Harry Crespi, and the detective mentioned the coincidence of someone else, here in this house, dying on the same day. From the description, it sounded like George Cravetz...so we decided to take a chance, and here we are."

"Yeah, here we are," Max complained. "I don't suppose you'd like to let us out of here."

"Before we do, I have another question." Michael was puzzled. Their story sounded straight, but why hadn't they brought the police in on this from the first. "You asked us not to call the police. Why? It seems to me that you'd want their help."

"Yes, well, that's another issue altogether," Charlie was pleased so far with the way things were going and police interference was the last thing he wanted. "Max and I are interested in getting the gold back into the vault without any fanfare."

"Why?" Addie asked.

Charlie nodded toward Max. "The two of us are responsible for the gold as part of our jobs, and it won't go well with the higher ups if they find out millions of dollars are missing."

"Bad for the bottom line," Max offered, "and bad for us. It could cost us our jobs."

"That's right. If we bring in the police, then the word gets out, and even if the gold is recovered, we'll still be at fault for letting it happen under our watch."

"Michael?" Addie questioned. "What do you think?"

After a minute Michael said, "Yes, we let them out."

Max was relieved. This was getting to him, stuck in this locker like they were.

"But we need to take a few minutes to explain all of this to Addie's aunts upstairs."

"Oh lord!" Addie realized that Helen and Rose were still in the dark about what was going on. "Yes, we certainly do." Then seeing the look on Max's face, she added "but it won't take long. We just want them to know that you're coming up. That it's ok."

Max just shook his head and sat down.

Helen and Rose had heard what was said and backed away from the basement door as Addie and Michael came up.

"You'll let them out, won't you?" asked Helen. "I shouldn't have locked them up."

"Well, Helen Whitaker!" Rose puffed up. "You did exactly the right thing! You had no idea if they were murderers or not!"

Addie gave Helen a quick hug. "Rose is right. You did the right thing...and it was a very brave thing to do."

"I'll say," Michael agreed. "Brave, *and* quick thinking."

"Well, I'll feel better when all of this is over." Helen still felt embarrassed that she had let them in the house in the first place.

Addie looked toward the basement and then back at Michael. "Do you believe them about the gold? Really, more to the point, do you believe their reason for not wanting the police called?"

Michael shrugged. "It seems plausible. I can see where an employer might be inclined to see this as gross incompetence. Losing that much money...over such a long period of time. Doesn't look good on your job performance report. By the way, they don't know for sure the gold is here."

"That's right!" Addie realized that the men never asked and that she and Michael never offered anything about the gold. It was obvious that this was the stolen gold. "We're talking about a fortune upstairs! Maybe this is a police matter."

"Oh, please don't call the police!" Rose startled them all with this plea. "I've been thinking about Mr. Barker and it just seems too bad to drag his name through all of this business."

"Well Rose..."Addie was amazed. "I think maybe Mr. Barker's name has got some baggage already. Let's see...he stole millions of dollars *and* he killed a man."

"That's just it. It wasn't really Mr. Barker who did all of that. It was Mr. Cavet or whatever his name was. Our Mr. Barker was a very different person. He was pleasant and reliable for all of these years and I think we should just let him rest in peace."

"It won't do any good to tell the police that he killed that man," Helen pointed out. "They're both dead so there is no one to arrest. And if we give all of that gold upstairs to these men and they put it back where it belongs, then Mr. Barker can rest in peace."

Addie couldn't argue with this logic. "What a good idea." She turned to Michael. "What do you think?"

He just grinned. "I think it's a plan. Mr. Barker's name is saved, the ill-gotten goods upstairs are disposed of, and the two men in the basement save their jobs. I don't see how it could get any better."

Once Max and Charlie had been released and Helen had stopped apologizing for incarcerating them, Addie explained that they were inclined to agree that there was no reason to call in the police.

"Oh yes, no police," said Rose. "You see we just feel that there would be no point. Mr. Barker is dead and it would only blacken his name if all of this came out."

The men had missed out on the conversation in which Mr. Barker's alter ego took the blame for the murder and robbery, so Rose's statement was somewhat confusing, but they were more than happy to agree.

"You won't have an argument from us on that point," Charlie began. "As we explained, we have a vested interest in getting the gold back to the casino without any notoriety."

"Oh yes!" Helen exclaimed. "You must take that gold and put it back! That will clear Mr. Barker's name once and for all."

"You can count on us for that," Max promised. He would believe their luck just as soon as he actually saw the gold. "Now...do you know where the gold is?"

"Oh yes. It's upstairs in Mr. Barker's room"

They all trooped up the stairs, down the hall and in to the bedroom. The afternoon sun cast shadows across the bed and onto the walls. Helen opened the windows to let in a little breeze and the song of the cicadas rose up on the air. The six stood for a moment without saying anything.

Max broke the silence. "This is it? The gold is here?" He looked at the dresser as a possible depository, but Addie shook her head.

"No, it's not in the dresser...not anywhere obvious. The fact is, it's all around us, but we might never have found it if it hadn't been for Michael." She picked up the carpenter's case and set it on the table. She fished around inside and pulled out the small plastic bag containing the piece of hardware that had led Michael to search for the secret panels. "Michael knew what this was," she said holding it up.

"What is it?" Max asked.

"It's a magnetic pressure latch," Michael explained. "They're usually used on doors or cabinets that don't have knobs. You push on the door and it releases the hold." He walked over by the wall. "He was paneling this room, not building cabinets, so the latch seemed out of place."

"It took him years," Addie offered. "He would work on it on the weekends that he was here and then in the summer he would spend the entire week on this project."

"He was so tidy about his work," Helen said. "He always cleaned up after himself. He said he didn't want to bother me with the dusting or sweeping up." She looked a little misty-eyed. "He was such a gentleman."

Rose put her arm around Helen, and then said to Michael, "Oh do show them what you found! It's just so clever."

Addie smiled. "Yes indeed, it was clever all around. Mr. Barker built a very clever hiding place, and Michael cleverly figured out where it was." She turned to him. "Go ahead. Show them."

He leaned down and pressed the corner of the panel and it swung open to reveal the trove of ill-gotten goods. Charlie went over and pried one of the bars out of its pocket.

"Well, I'll be goddamned!" He quickly counted the remaining bars. "Twenty!" Then looking around he asked, "Are these panels all like this?"

"Every one," confirmed Addie. "And mostly full." She went around the room opening the panels. "There are fourteen in all and they can each hold twenty bars." She had reached the end of the panels that were full. "So you can see that twelve are full...that's two hundred and forty, plus eleven more in this thirteenth panel...so that's two hundred and fifty-one all together." She looked at Charlie and Max who were gazing in amazement at the sight before them. "Gold bars," she said, "two hundred and fifty-one gold bars," in case they had missed her meaning. "But it looks like he planned to take two hundred and eighty bars altogether."

Max looked at Charlie, "I thought you said there were two hundred sixty bars missing."

"That's what I thought." Charlie could have been off when he was weighing the bars. He had worked quickly not wanting to attract anyone's attention. "Maybe I miscounted. But the bulk of it seems to be here."

"How did he get away with all of this?" Michael was puzzled. "It seems like it would be noticeable...that many bars disappearing."

"He switched them out with fake bars, which I must say look like the real thing. The weight is slightly different though, which is why I first suspected something. I got a scale and weighed them, all two hundred and ninety-nine bars. I came up with two hundred and sixty fakes...at least I thought it was two hundred and sixty. I could have been off." Charlie shook his head, "What a plan...he was going to keep this up for quite awhile if he was actually going to fill up all of these panels." He looked around at the gaping doors. "He must have planned to leave the top bars alone."

"The top bars?" Addie asked.

"The kilo bars are in the vault, of course, but they're stacked on a cart in six rows, five deep, ten in a stack. The ones on top are still real. He was taking from the bottom and he must have planned to leave real ones on the top...when he decided that he had enough and quit."

Max looked around the room. He was ready to go. "This is a lot here. This will take care of things at the casino."

"You're right. This is good." Good, it was better than good and it was time to clear out. It seemed as if there would be no argument from these people. "We have to pack this up somehow." He looked at Helen, "I don't suppose you'd sell us a few of those suitcases we've been locked up with, would you?"

"Oh, my word!" She was quite contrite. "You just take whatever you need."

"Yes, indeed," chimed in Rose. "We're just glad to see the last of this business. It's been such a strange experience. We just want to be finished with it. Am I right?" she questioned Addie.

"You are very right, Rose." She turned to Charlie. "How are you taking this back to Las Vegas? You can't fly."

"That's right," said Charlie. "We couldn't go through security with this even if we could lift it. It's really heavy...all of this must be close to five hundred pounds."

"Maybe you should think about Brinks," said Michael. "This is millions of dollars you're packing up."

"I thought about that, but it will attract too much attention. Max and I just hope to get all of this back into the vault without any fanfare. We can drive it back. We have a rented car and we'll just drive straight through. It's a long drive but we can spell each other."

"Yeah, we'll be fine," Max piped up. "We just need those suitcases."

"Oh, let me go get them," offered Helen.

"I'll help," said Max, and he followed her out of the room.

They finally decided on one large suitcase, which would fit all of the bars. But, of course, they couldn't lift it. So they put the suitcase in the trunk of the car and then made a series of trips, up and down the stairs, in and out of the house, using several smaller bags. Charlie insisted on paying for the luggage. They would keep the smaller cases also, to use to empty the large one.

As they were getting into the car, Addie asked, "What if we need to get in touch with you...do we just call the casino?"

Charlie hesitated for a moment, and then said, "I'll give you my cell phone. That's a better way to reach me." He didn't want them calling the casino.

"I was just thinking that if we find those other bars..."

"Yes, well...if you do, call me here." He handed her a slip of paper that he had used to jot down the number. "I could have been wrong about the number missing." He slipped into the car behind the steering wheel, turned the key, and put the car into gear. Max rolled down his window and gave the group a high five. Then they pulled away from the house and disappeared down the street.

"I have the most ridiculous feeling...it's like we are waving family off on a vacation, not sending two strangers off with millions of dollars in the trunk of their car." She gave a worried look at Michael. "Do you think we did the right thing?"

"Do you regret giving them the gold?" he asked.

"Oh, no!" Rose jumped in, "I'm sure we did just the right thing. That gold just brings bad luck with it."

"I didn't mean you should have kept the gold," Michael smiled. "I'm just wondering if it might have been better to call the police in to all of this."

"Then those nice men would have lost their jobs!" Helen was shocked at the thought.

"No, I'm glad we didn't call the police," Addie confessed. "That would have made all of this more complicated...if that's possible."

"Ok then," Michael offered, "we did the right thing. Now back to reality?"

"Whatever that is!" Addie laughed.

"Now, Michael, say you'll stay for dinner," Rose insisted starting back up the steps to the house.

"Oh yes, Michael, you have to stay for dinner," Helen agreed. "I have the nicest roast and it's much too big for the three of us."

"You got me," he laughed and gave Addie a wink.

Charlie had just turned the corner and was headed to the interstate when Max said, "I got something to show you. Something I picked up at the house."

"What's that?" Charlie was concentrating on the GPS directions leading them out of town. He was still having a hard time believing their luck. This whole thing might just work. "You picked up something?" He glanced over at Max and was surprised to see him holding a gun...not by the grip though, by the barrel. "What the hell?"

"Yeah, well I saw this on the dining room table when we were getting the bags and I decided it would make things more even between us, if you know what I mean."

Charlie snorted, "I know what you mean. Max, you're nobody's fool."

"I take that as a compliment," Max said sliding the gun back into his jacket pocket. "Now, where are we going?"

"I thought Denver would be good. We'll get there early morning, there will be plenty of self-storage places, and we can fly out late afternoon."

"Denver it is."

Chapter 16

Las Vegas
The trip to Denver from Kansas City went without a hitch. It was an all night drive on a highway that was as straight as an arrow and would have generated a dangerous sense of monotony had they not been high on the euphoria of greed. The gold in the trunk buoyed them up and gave them an adrenalin rush that made sleep impossible. They still found it hard to believe that they had pulled this off. The fact that they were able to drive away without an alarm being raised seemed improbable, and for the first few hours they fully expected to see flashing red lights coming up fast behind them. But they didn't. They kept their speed just at the limit and gradually began to believe in their luck. They stopped for gas and to use the john twice, agreeing that the one who went in to the bathroom took the car keys with them, a sensible precaution.

They arrived in the Denver area far too early for any public storage company office to be open, so they killed time with food. They were ravenous and loaded up with takeout from a fast food chain, and then drove to a rest stop area along the highway. It gave them time to do an Internet search for storage companies in the vicinity of the Denver airport. They had agreed that they needed two places, that it would look odd if they rented two units in the same facility, and they each needed a unit of their own for obvious reasons. It all went so smoothly that they were at the airport by ten o'clock. Because Max was headed to corporate headquarters back east for his review, and he didn't want to leave a trail from Denver, he booked a ticket that would take him to Newark and from there he would get a flight to Philadelphia.

That way the Denver connection would be hard to trace. Charlie booked a ticket to Las Vegas that left within the hour and would get him there in order to go into the casino at his usual time.

The phone rang as soon as Charlie walked into the office. It was Tom Woods.

"Glad you're back Mr. Black. Security just let me know you were in the building."

"What's up Tom?"

"It's about George Cravetz."

Charlie tensed. "What about him? Is he back?"

"No, I'm afraid not." Tom hesitated. "Is it ok if I come up to your office to talk about this?"

"Sure, come on." Charlie hung up the phone and tried to quiet the apprehension that was beginning to build. Any mention of Cravetz made him uneasy.

Tom looked worried as he came into Charlie's office.

"What's the matter Tom? Sit down."

"They found George's car at the airport." Tom handed a paper to Charlie.

"What's this?" He could see it was a report of some kind.

"It's basically a receipt for George's car. It's from an impound yard. His car was cited as abandoned at an airport parking lot and towed. The yard called the office after they got no response at George's house. I'm not sure how they tracked him to us, but they did."

"Boy, that's strange. The airport?"

Tom Woods shook his head. "I don't know what to think. He wouldn't have gone to Kansas City. Mr. Grenwald made the delivery this past weekend."

"Have you reported this to the police?" Charlie wasn't sure he wanted to get the police involved, but it would look odd if he didn't seem concerned.

"No, that's what I wanted to talk to you about. I think we should file a missing person report. I'm really afraid something bad has happened."

"Like what?"

"Well, unless George suddenly took it into his head to go on a trip, which is entirely unlike him, I think someone stole his car and left it at the Las Vegas airport."

"You're right, we need to call the police in on this." Charlie began to think this might be a fortunate turn of events for the explanation of George's disappearance.

"If someone took his car when he was camping, and stranded him out there in the desert... after all this time and no word..." Tom's thought trailed off.

"He could be dead." Charlie finished it for him. "You're right. We would have heard something by now if he'd been found." He reached for the phone. "He could even be dead in his house. When I went out there his car was missing from the garage. Maybe the theft happened there and his body's inside." He dialed the police, again pleased with the way things were going.

The police were sufficiently interested to send two detectives to the casino to take a report. They talked to both Charlie and Tom and other people in the accounting department, which caused Miss Alcott to begin weeping for poor Mr. Cravetz. They sent a patrol car to George's house and the officers were able to gain entry through the back door, but found the house empty. They checked with the airlines, but there was no trace of a George Cravetz booking a ticket in the time frame that they were investigating. Without any more information about where

George might have gone camping, the investigation was stymied. It was a damn big desert when you didn't have a starting point.

The case remained on the police books as unsolved for the better part of the year, and, in time, George's disappearance became one of those quirky stories repeated at the water cooler.

"You don't think this police search is going to end up in Kansas City, do you?" Max had returned from his 'review' in Philadelphia and was met with his share of questions from the detectives about George.

"No, I don't think there's any reason for them to look in that direction," Charlie reassured him. "Everybody here is sure he went to the desert. Even if it did go to KC, it would dead-end with our Vegas connection." He looked out of the window of Max's office to the distant edge of the city and the beginning of the vast desert. "I'm feeling pretty good about this, Max. If this goes like I hope, George will be explained away, and no one will connect him to the gold...or to us, for that matter. Now tell me, how did it go with Giamacchi?"

"Just like you said. Everyone was so appreciative of my long years of service...yadda, yadda, yadda." Max leaned back in his chair and pulled an envelope out of his inside breast pocket. "Look, they gave me a certificate to prove it." He unfolded a packet of papers and waved them in Charlie's direction.

"That's a certificate?"

"The same thing. It's the details of my early retirement package. Because I'm such a *treasure*, I get one year's salary and some stock options in the business. I told them I'd rather cash out the stocks. I'd like to use the money for a vacation." He folded the papers and put them back in the envelope. "If you hadn't given me a head's up Charlie, I would probably have had a coronary. Anybody could see I was getting the bum's rush. But, you know what? It's enough money to make the travel plans I have look reasonable."

"I'd ask where you were going, but it's not a good idea for me to know." They had agreed that the less they knew about each others plans, the better for both of them.

Charlie organized a large party to celebrate Max's retirement and to introduce the new boss, Phil Barcone. It was a glittery party, and included many of the other Las Vegas casino managers, and even some of the city council. Max was genuinely touched. He promised to stay connected with everyone, although he mentioned doing some traveling. He said he had put it off all of these years and was now going to make up for lost time. Everyone wished him well, especially Charlie. The two men drank a toast to George as the last guest left for the evening.

Max sent a few sporadic postcards to show that he was true to his word, and they were shared around the office. But eventually, as with most retirees, Max was forgotten and business moved on.

AnneDavid

October 2013

Chapter 17

A few days after Max left, Charlie got a call to report to Mr. Barcone's office.

"Charlie, I want you to start an audit of the books. I'll need to send a report to the head office soon. We'll get an outside accounting firm to do the work, of course."

"Of course." Charlie was prepared for this. He had already alerted Tom Woods to have the books ready, but he wanted to keep the gold out of the accounting process. "We have a pretty unusual account here that you need to know about. You may not want to include it in the general audit."

"What do you mean?" Barcone gave him a puzzled look.

"It's an account that's never been on the public books, as far as I know."

"What are you talking about?"

"If you have a few minutes, why don't I show you?"

Charlie had committed the combination to the gold safe to memory when he weighed the kilo bars. Now he spun the dial, opened the door, and rolled out the gold laden cart for Barcone's inspection.

"Holy crap! Is this gold?" Barcone was astounded.

"It is, and at twelve hundred dollars an ounce, based on the present market, it's probably worth in the neighborhood of twelve million dollars, and that's just the kilo bars. When you figure in the big bars and the coins, it's considerably more."

"You say this isn't on the public books?"

"It's not...I don't know how long this stuff has been here...there doesn't seem to be any history to it, and there sure aren't any official books to show. The accounting department has kept an unofficial monthly report for the last twenty plus years, but it was never included in the regular report." Charlie went on when it was obvious that Barcone was at a loss for words. "Every once in awhile there's a customer who wants to take their winnings in gold, or wants to use gold to buy chips, and the management has accommodated them, but I think it's a bad idea."

"Why?"

"It leaves us open to some disgruntled gambler accusing us of palming off a fake bar and demanding cash. In fact, that just happened to Max. He paid the guy off because he didn't want to get the police involved, but he had no way to tell if the bar came from the casino or not."

"He shouldn't have paid."

"Maybe not, but the publicity would have been bad. It could have alerted the IRS to the fact that we have this stockpile. I know for a fact that as long as I've been here we've never paid taxes on it, if they were due that is. No one wants to rock the boat by asking."

"I can see that's a problem. What are you thinking?"

Charlie took a gamble. "Maybe we should sell it. Of course the price just dipped recently...and there are financial predictions that it could go as high as five thousand dollars an ounce in the near future..."

Barcone took the bait. "There's no need to rush to sell. It's better to wait and get top dollar."

"Fine, I'll just lock it up again and you can deal with it later." The fact that Barcone didn't ask if the head office knew about this, or mention informing them about it, wasn't lost on Charlie. He felt sure that when the problem with the gold was discovered, if it ever was, he would be long gone and Barcone would be left to explain. However, he suspected that Barcone would be more likely to keep the information to himself. After all, as far as Barcone was concerned, all of the gold in the safe was genuine. Quite a temptation.

Before he left for good, though, there were several loose ends that Charlie needed to clean up, or maybe loose 'cannons' was a better term. There were other people at the casino that knew about the gold. Who knew what problems could arise from office talk about George and the gold account. Tom Woods, Mildred Alcott, and the security guard all had stories to tell. He picked up a stack of files and headed into Barcone's office.

"You said you wanted to go over these personnel records, so I hope this is a good time to start."

"Charlie, come on in." Barcone was hanging up the phone. "I was just talking to one of my staff back in Atlantic City. Good man and I'd like to get him out here, so this is a perfect time to start thinking about how we're going forward with personnel here." He stopped to uncap a bottle of expensive water. "I don't know what it is, but I'm always thirsty. Living in the desert, I guess. Now let's see what you've got."

Charlie spread the files out on the desk. "These are the different departments, and there are run downs on each of the people in them...basically a condensed record of performance reviews. What department would this person be working into?"

"Accounting. He was head of accounting in Atlantic City and I'd like for him to take over that position here. I understand the head accountant here is gone?"

Charlie nodded his head. "Yes, he is." He hoped he wouldn't be asked where. But Barcone obviously didn't care, so long as his man was in.

"Great, then that's settled. But we need to take a serious look at the overall numbers. Personnel cost money, you know, and this casino has a bloated staff. I want you to see what you can do to cut back, but still run efficiently. It's all about the bottom line." He stopped to take another pull at the water bottle. "I trust your judgment. Come up with some recommendations, just make sure we don't run into any EEOC problems, and then run them by me."

"Will do."

Charlie was thorough. He went through each department looking for candidates for early retirement packages. As a culling strategy it was a win-win situation. Those employees left willingly and no replacement was needed. Mildred Alcott was one of those individuals. She wasn't really eligible for an early retirement offer, and the woman from personnel, who sat in on these conferences with the employees, was quite opposed to it. But Charlie ignored her protests and made the offer anyway. Miss Alcott seemed very surprised, but said that she had been considering retirement for some time, now that Mr. Cravetz was gone. She seemed grateful for the offer. One cannon down, two to go.

The security guard turned out to be a non-issue. Soon after Max left he resigned to go with another casino that could offer him a better benefit package. That left Tom, and Barcone unwittingly helped Charlie deal with that. He knew Tom was disappointed when he heard that he wasn't going to be made head of the department. When George hadn't returned he must have hoped the job would go to him. Charlie began to put out feelers to his counterparts in the many other gambling establishments in the area, and, not surprisingly, found several opportunities for Tom. Now, with Tom Woods as the head of the accounting department at a casino at the other end of The

Strip, there was only one item left on Charlie's check list - a plausible reason for him to leave Las Vegas, and that reason had just arrived in the mail. He smiled as he pulled the letter of interest from the stack on his desk. It was a job offer from a large financial firm in Boston and his ticket out of Las Vegas. It would allow him to leave without causing suspicion. Charlie pocketed the job offer, which he actually planned to turn down, and called Barcone's office to request a few minutes with the boss.

"Damn, Charlie, I'm sorry to see you go. We were just beginning to roll here."

"Thanks, Phil. I appreciate that." Charlie held up the letter. "This offer is just too good to pass up. It puts me on a fast track to upper management. And...it gets me back to the East Coast." He smiled ruefully.

"You got family there?"

"Some. It'll be good to be closer."

"Well, if there is ever anything I can do...just let me know." Barcone had come around his desk and had his arm around Charlie's shoulders. "We'll miss you here."

As Charlie left the office he could almost imagine that he heard Barcone putting in a call to his Atlantic City assistant manager telling him to report to Las Vegas. No one would miss him...and that was good.

As he cleaned out his office, packing up the few personal items that were there in a casino promotional bag, he allowed the one remaining potential snag to come up front and center. It concerned him that the people in Kansas City knew the whole story. Well, not the part about Denver, but if they ever contacted the casino the rest of the story could come out.

But the only reason that they might try to get in touch would be because they found more gold. He thought there were nine additional kilo bars missing, but there was no way to check that out without weighing all of the bars in the safe again. So he could be wrong about the number. But even if he wasn't wrong, and they found the gold, maybe human nature would prevail and they would decide not to call. That was probably a remote possibility considering they seemed over the moon in the honesty department. But it *had* been six months and they hadn't called yet, so, as much as Charlie disliked the idea of a loose end, he would have to let it go. He checked the time. His flight left in two hours. He was moving on, first stop Denver and then off to parts unknown.

April 2014

Chapter 18

Grimaud
Cote d'Azure
France

From the terrace of the villa, Berenice watched the blue Fiat wind its way up the hill from the town of Grimaud. She had been sent by the agency to open up the house before the new owner arrived. And while she hoped this might work out to be a permanent housekeeping position, she felt some trepidation about working for an American. Her experience was that they could be a trifle gauche, not a quality admired in France. But the car was a good sign, sensible for these roads. She went inside and through the house to open the front door.

There was a satisfying crunch to the gravel as the car turned in through the gates to the driveway in front of the house. It was a lovely house, a villa according to the real estate brochure, with bougainvillea climbing the stone walls and spilling over the red tiled eaves. A small fountain stood to one side of the drive with a nymph of some sort pouring water from a pitcher into the pool.

As the car came to a stop, Berenice came down the steps to open the door and welcome the American. "Bonjour, Madam, welcome to Villa Tournesol."

"Bonjour...Berenice? Is that right?"

"Oui, Madam." She stood back to allow the woman to get out of the car, a middle aged woman, not beautiful, but quite striking with short silver gray hair, wearing tailored sports clothes, and just the right amount of tasteful jewelry. Berenice was hopeful about this situation.

"The agent said that you speak English."

"Oui...yes, Madam. I am fluent in English."

"Oh good, and I want you to help me become fluent in French. I know a little, just enough to get me into trouble I think, but if I'm going to live here I need to do better."

Berenice was sure that this would work out. "Madam, can I show you the house?"

"Oh yes! I've been waiting for this for a long time."

It had been years and, at first, was only a wistful thought. But as time passed and she saw that her funding source was secure, the thought became a plan, one that would become the focus of her life. Besides the money, other things began to fall into place that made moving to Europe possible. An interest piece in the newspaper one Sunday morning caught her eye, an article extolling the deep satisfaction from discovering your 'roots.' People were becoming more interested all the time in tracing their heritage, and some even went so far as to apply for dual citizenship in countries that offered that to American citizens. Ireland was one of those countries.

According to the article, all it took was having a parent or grandparent born there, and her grandfather came from County Cork so why shouldn't she explore that possibility. It took some time to gather all of the documentation needed, but she had time. In the end she received an Irish passport and became a citizen in the European Union at the same time. Buying property in any of the EU countries became just a matter of money and that was piling up rather briskly.

The fact that she was actually here, standing at the front door of her own house, *villa,* was an unimaginable scenario all those years ago when her husband left her. He had taken what cash they had, and the car, and disappeared never to be heard from again. She had nothing, with the exception of an over abundance of low self-esteem and rent to pay. She had to get a job. The one that she found paid just enough to take care of her rent and her other very basic needs. She rode the bus to work each day, packed a sandwich that she ate at her desk, and saved up enough money to get a divorce. She didn't mention it to anyone at work because she was embarrassed. They were nice people, but she didn't want them feeling sorry for her behind her back. It was easier for people to think she was an old maid instead of a jilted wife. She didn't change her name, that would give her away, and so she remained Mildred Alcott.

February 1998

Chapter 19

Las Vegas

She had a certificate from a local business school in bookkeeping and was able to find work at one of the large casinos in their accounting department. The job was routine, bordering on mind numbing even, but it helped her regain some of her self-respect. Earning enough money to pay her bills and set a little aside through careful penny pinching gave her hope that better days were ahead. She wasn't sure what better looked like, but it wasn't where she had been.

The office staff was surprisingly large. There were a lot of financial transactions that occurred in a large casino, payroll and general number crunching among them, and she was in the number crunching department along with three or four other people, depending on the season. At tax time, part-time help was brought in. But regularly, every day, there were three of them, Mr. Cravetz, head accountant, Mr. Woods, his assistant, and her. Mr. Woods was a pleasant man, making sure that she understood all of the systems that they used, giving a little advice about which benefit package she might want to choose, little every day things. Mr. Cravetz, on the other hand, said very little to her, or anyone else for that matter. He seemed painfully shy. He rarely made any conversation and when he did have something to say about things other than work, they always seemed odd. He asked her once if she enjoyed typing. When she said yes she did, what could you say to something like that, he said he thought so because she seemed to be quite good at it. So she was slightly alarmed when he approached her desk one morning and asked if he could speak with her.

"Of course, Mr. Cravetz." She hoped he wasn't dissatisfied with her work. She needed this job. She followed him to his desk.

"Miss Alcott, you've been here almost a month and I'm glad to say that you seem to be working out in this department." He wasn't looking directly at her, more at her neck.

"Thank you, Mr. Cravetz. I enjoy being here." She almost added that she still liked typing, too.

"There is one more responsibility that goes with your job that I want to tell you about, and I feel sure that you will be up to it."

Maybe it meant more money?

Cravetz cleared his throat and continued. "Each month I go to the vault and take possession of a large amount of money which I must deliver to Kansas City, and I also do a reconciling of another account that is under our department's supervision. I always have a security guard and another person from this department with me as a safety measure."

Was this going to be dangerous?

"The person that you replaced was the one who accompanied me, but now that will be your responsibility."

Probably not more money.

"We will open a large safe within the vault in order to do our work. I have one part of the combination and you will have the other part which you must keep locked in your desk at all times." He stopped and glanced up toward her face to see if she was taking in all of this.

"Of course, Mr. Cravetz. I appreciate the trust you put in me." She thought that sounded corny but he seemed pleased to hear her say it.

"Yes...well today is the day. I always go to the vault at exactly ten o'clock on the last Friday of the month. " He looked up at the wall clock. "It's nine-thirty so you'll need to be ready in half an hour. Mr. Woods has the folder that you'll need locked in his desk and he's expecting you to ask for it."

When he didn't say anything else, Mildred thanked him and walked over to Mr. Woods' desk. The three of them were within the sound of a normal conversation so this whole thing seemed farcical.

"Mr. Cravetz says I'm to ask you for the folder."

Tom Woods gave her a wink and then solemnly unlocked his desk drawer and pulled out a black folder and handed it across to her. "I'm glad to turn this over to you Miss Alcott. I'm sure it is in good hands now."

"Thank you, Mr. Woods." She accepted the folder and hurried back to her desk. What in the world was this about? Obviously, Mr. Woods didn't think it was as serious as Mr. Cravetz did. She dutifully put the folder in her top desk drawer and fished the little key out of the pencil well and locked it. She looked around for someplace to put the key, and settled on the small coin purse in her handbag. She glanced up and caught the look of approval on Mr. Cravetz' face.

At exactly two minutes to ten, Mr. Cravetz took a similar black folder from a locked drawer, stood up, retrieved his suit jacket from the coat tree behind his desk, put it on, and approached her desk.

"It's time to go to the vault," he announced, as if she might have missed the significance of his movements.

"Yes Mr. Cravitz. I'm ready." She had retrieved the folder from her desk when she saw him making his preparations, and, by the way, she could see that it was ten o'clock. She soon learned that this was the ritual that was performed each month. He was not only a creature of habit; he was *the* creature of habit. It was a quality that she came to count on. But on this particular Friday morning it was her first visit to the vault, so his manner just seemed odd.

They stopped at the guard desk in front of the vault and each signed in on a visitor sheet. One of the guards at the desk took a set of keys from a drawer and stood up.

"Good morning Mr. Cravetz. It's the end of the month already? Time sure flies when you're having fun." He seemed to think this quite funny.

"Good morning Henry," and George Cravetz permitted himself to smile at the little joke. "Yes, it's time to get the delivery together and take care of the other business."

They followed Henry through the massive open door into the vault and through to a barred gate that had to be unlocked. Inside there was a table and several other large safes. One was open and there were trays of cash visible on the shelves. The other safes were closed. The guard locked the barred gate behind them.

"Shall we take care of the cash first, Henry?"

"Yes sir, Mr. Cravetz," and Henry pulled a tray of banded bills off of a shelf and put it on the table. Mr. Cravetz produced a voucher signed by the managing director of the casino, and he proceeded to count out the amount indicated and then signed for the cash. He directed Henry and Miss Alcott to verify the amount and then sign also. The guard produced an empty brief case and Mr. Cravetz packed the cash inside.

"I'll pick this up at the usual time, Henry." Then he glanced toward Mildred and explained, "I am entrusted with this monthly payment which goes to casino investors in Kansas City. I'm allowed to leave at noon in order to make a flight that gets me there by five o'clock. That way it's part of my working day."

Mildred soon found out that those were the only hours that he was ever away from the office during a working day. In fact, she learned that he had never missed a day, or was late in all of the years that he had worked for the casino.

"And now," he went on, "I take care of another of my responsibilities." It almost seemed as if his chest puffed out as he stepped over to one of the large locked safes. He opened his folder and withdrew a slip of paper from an envelope attached to the inside cover, and started to input the numbers on the dial of a safe, when he hesitated. "Miss Alcott, if you'll just turn around. That way you won't see my numbers." She did as she was asked and he returned to the lock and finished his part, and then stood back. "Now, Miss Alcott, it's your turn."

She opened her folder and saw that she had the same kind of envelope inside, also containing a slip of paper.

"It's the other half of the combination," he said. "For security reasons, no one person has the whole combination. If you'll just put in your part...I won't look."

She stepped up to the door and carefully followed the number sequence on her paper. When she finished she stepped back and George Cravetz turned the handle and opened the door. He paused for a moment, and then rolled a cart out and over to the table. Mildred wasn't sure what she was looking at. Then Mr. Cravetz solemnly explained, "This is the store of casino gold and our department is in charge of the bookwork involved with it."

"Oh my, that's a lot of gold!" She couldn't help the comment. Of course, she'd never seen anything like it and her obvious amazement seemed to please Mr. Cravetz because he allowed himself a small smile...of what? Satisfaction? Pride?

"Yes, quite a responsibility as you can see." He pulled a ledger off of a shelf in the safe and opened it out on the table. "I make an inventory of this gold each month and record it in this ledger."

She couldn't think what to say.

"While it's quite infrequent, customers of the casino sometimes prefer to deal in gold rather than currency, so we have this store to accommodate them...coins, kilo bars, and two four hundred ounce bars."

"Do all of the casinos have gold like this?"

"I'm not familiar with the practices of the other casinos," his tone was quite prim. "I only know that this is what we do. The store of gold was here long before I came. It's accounting was entrusted to me when I became the head of the department."

"Oh yes, I see." She could feel the reprove in his voice. "When I took over this responsibility there had never been a regular inventory made, it was only done sporadically. I instituted a regular monthly accounting regime. I feel that you can't be too careful with other peoples' money." He turned back to the cart and began inspecting the contents. "This doesn't take long at all." He picked up a clear plastic sleeve containing coins, opened it, tipped the coins into his palm, counted them, returned them to the case, and noted it in the ledger. "You see? Only a few seconds." He quickly finished with the coins and then turned to the kilo bars. He took each stack from the cart and placed it on the table, counting as he went. "Three hundred in all," he said, writing that figure in the ledger, and then placing all of the bars neatly back on the cart. "There's no need to move the large bars as there are only two and we can all see that." Again it went into the book. "Alright Henry, if I can just get you to sign the ledger under today's date."

Henry stepped up to the book and duly signed the page. "Nice work, Mr. Cravetz. You're real efficient."

"Thank you, Henry. Now Miss Alcott...if you will sign." Henry handed her the pen and turned the book toward her. She leaned over, signed, and gave the pen back to Henry.

"Thanks Miss. I guess you're the new person in accounting?"

"Yes."

"Then I expect I'll see you next month."

"That's right Henry." Mr. Cravetz collected his folder, where he had also recorded the same figures that went into the vault ledger, and stepped over to the locked gate. "Miss Alcott will be coming with me from now on."

"Alright, sir." He unlocked the gate and they stepped out. "I guess you'll pick up the money case on your way out as usual?" They had left the briefcase containing the cash on the table inside the locked room.

"Yes, I'll pick it up at one o'clock. Promptly."

"Yes sir. You're always right on time."

"Ducks in a row, Henry, ducks in a row."

Later in the afternoon, after Mr. Cravetz had left for Kansas City, one of the women who worked in payroll stopped by her desk. She reminded Mildred of a tomato, round, favoring bright red clothing, and of all things, green spiky hair.

"Welcome to the department."

"Thank you."

"Yeah, I hope things go ok for you. You look like you fit in here."

Mildred wasn't sure if this was a compliment or not. "Yes, I'm feeling more comfortable every day. I don't see why it won't work out."

"Well...not everyone can work with Mr. Cravetz. He's a real stickler for routine...his *and* yours." She looked over at Tom Woods. "I'm right aren't I, Mr. Woods."

"Now Angie, Mr. Cravetz is just making sure that all of the work is done well."

"Yeah, well he'd drive me batty with all of his *routines*." She looked back at Mildred, "He's had a few people bail out on him. That's all I'm saying."

"Yes, thank you. I don't mind routines." It made her uneasy to talk about Mr. Cravetz this way when he wasn't here. "I'm sure I'll get used to his." She wished the tomato would go away.

"Ok, don't say I didn't warn you." She walked off toward her department but tossed one last comment over her shoulder. "You can always come to payroll, if it gets to you here."

"Thanks Angie," said Tom Woods, "but that's not very productive." They watched Angie roll on down the aisle and then he said to Mildred. "Don't mind her. I don't know if she thinks she's being funny or helpful, but don't pay any attention to that stuff about George. Mr. Cravetz. He does have his routines and he likes it in others. It's the nature of this business. Every number needs its own little box. That's what makes him good at his work. Don't listen to Angie, you'll do fine here."

"Thank you, I appreciate that. I like routines," she said again. "I know what to expect." What she really liked at this point was the job, so if it meant putting up with Mr. Cravetz' routines, she would do it."

"He's a nice man, just a little fussy," said Mr. Woods turning back to his computer.

As time went by she discovered the routines. He arrived in the office each morning promptly at eight a.m., took off his jacket - he always wore a suit and tie even in the hot Nevada summer - hung the jacket on the coat tree behind his desk, laid out his ledgers and pencils and sat down to work. Whenever he left the office, whether to get his lunch, go to the restroom, consult with management, or make a trip to the vault, he put on his jacket. And, he took it off and hung it up when he came back. She heard from the tomato, who had it from a friend that worked in a restaurant in the main part of the casino where Mr. Cravetz ate lunch, that he always ordered a plain turkey sandwich, a cup of fruit, and a glass of ice tea. Every day. It never varied. So she wasn't surprised when the second trip to the vault was a carbon copy of the first time. Even the small talk was the same.

It was during the third month's trip that she noticed they were *all* doing things in the exact same way, from standing in the same places, to doing things in the same order, as if they were in a curious little one act play and Mr. Cravetz was the director and star. The only thing that varied was the amount of cash counted out each month, but even that was handled in the same way. There was no variation in the accounting of the gold because there weren't any transactions that had taken place during the three months since she had been there to warrant an adjustment in the books.

As they were making the vault journey on the morning of the fourth month, Mildred got up the courage to ask a question.

" Mr. Cravetz, I was just wondering..."

"Yes, Miss Alcott?" He was pushing the elevator button, but glanced over at her shoulder.

"Well, in the last three months there haven't been any transactions in the gold account, but you always inventory the whole stock. Are you worried that some might be missing?"

"Oh no. I'm sure that could never happen. We...you and I are the only ones with the combination. No. No one would be able to get into the safe. Whenever the management wants to handle a gold request for a patron, they have to ask for our help. So we know when there is a transaction."

"I see." She hesitated to ask any more questions, but now she really wondered why he did it. If he knew there would be nothing different, it seemed like a waste of time... so inefficient... something that was out of character for him. He couldn't be so fanatical about routine that he went through this whole process in order to be *ready* to adjust the books when he had to, could he?

He stopped just before they went into the vault room. "I have a little secret to confide, Miss Alcott."

He was smiling rather nervously she thought, but it was making her nervous that he wanted to 'confide' something in her.

"It's really quite silly," he went on. "I just find it rather thrilling to be able to handle so much money." He gave a nervous little laugh. "Of course I'll never have anything like the amount of wealth on that cart, but at least once a month I can count it out and stack it back up." He paused. "It's really very satisfying."

"Oh, yes. I can see that it would be." There was a name for things like this...what was it...psychosis, neurosis, dementia...

"I hope this can be our little secret. I wouldn't want people to think I was..."

"Of course not, Mr. Cravetz. I would never mention this to anyone." He seemed to be waiting for something more. "Never. It's department business and I never discuss that with anyone...not even Mr. Woods."

That seemed to satisfy him and he nodded and opened the door to the vault room.

Now that she knew why he counted the kilo bars each time, Mildred noticed that he did indeed seem to take great pleasure from the experience. He would carefully replace all of the bars on the cart, reverently – she thought that word hit the nail on the head – and then push the cart back into the safe, stand back, put his hands in his suit coat pockets, thumbs out and give a sigh of satisfaction. He stood ramrod straight with his small chest puffed out, obviously enjoying this brush with wealth. Then he would return to reality and have them sign the ledger. It was just like a ballet, the same pas de trois preformed monthly, and they were all quite good in their roles. Henry knew when to open a lock or hand out a pen, she was quite good at taking her cues from both men about where to stand and when to sign, and Mr. Cravetz excelled in the role of premier danseur. She didn't know why the metaphor of a ballet occurred to her. They weren't particularly graceful, but she did think that they might all at once be inspired to do little leaps – jetes? – as they exited the vault.

It was only in month six that she noticed something else. It could have been her imagination playing tricks on her, but when

Mr. Cravetz completed the move of pushing the cart back into the safe and placing his hands in his pockets she thought she saw a small jerk, or slight sagging of the left hand pocket. She watched for it in month seven and there it was. What did it mean?

The more she thought about it the more she wondered if he was putting something in his pocket. Of course the only thing handy at that moment was one of the kilo bars, but that seemed preposterous. She must be wrong. But then ... if she could just see the inside of his pocket...highly unlikely because his jacket was either on his body or hanging on the coat tree behind his desk, and he never went anywhere without putting it back on.

Chapter 20

She had just come into the office one morning and was settling into her desk, putting her purse in a drawer, opening up her computer, checking the time - she liked to be early - when Mr. Woods came through the door with a cardboard nursery flat full of green plants.

"Good morning Miss Alcott." He was obviously pleased with himself this morning. He set the box on his desk. "You're early as usual, and Mr. Cravetz should be here right about..." he looked at the clock, "now."

The door opened just as the minute hand worked its way to the twelve and Mr. Cravetz appeared on cue.

"Good morning Miss Alcott, good morning Tom." Mildred wondered how long she had to work there before anyone called her by her first name.

"Good morning, Mr. Cravetz."

"Good morning, George."

"My word, Tom, what have we here? It looks like a garden on your desk."

"My wife and I were at the nursery this weekend and they were having a terrific sale on house plants and she suggested I bring some to the office. What do you think?" He looked at them expectantly.

"I don't mind, Tom. But I don't have much of a green thumb, I'm afraid."

"I don't mind caring for them," Mildred ventured. "I'm usually good with plants."

"No allergics anyone?" Tom Woods inquired and Mildred and Mr. Cravetz both said no. "Then good. Can I turn them over to you Miss Alcott? You can spruce us up." He moved the box of plants to her desk.

"Well, they'll need light, of course." She looked at the obvious source of daylight in the office, the windowsill directly behind Mr. Cravetz desk. "Let's see..." she poked around the plants. There were eight in the box. "I could put one on each of our desks and put the rest on the windowsill." She looked at Mr. Cravetz to see how this idea was going over and when he didn't object she went on. "Then perhaps I could rotate the plants each week so that they all get their share of the sunlight."

"There, Miss Alcott, I knew you'd be on top of it." Tom Woods went back to his desk and settled in for the morning.

"Yes, that will be just fine, Miss Alcott. Thank you for stepping up." Mr. Cravetz turned his attention from horticulture back to his daily routine.

Mildred chose three plants for their desks, and then placed the other five on the windowsill, the one directly behind Mr. Cravetz' desk *and* next to the coat tree. She could hardly contain her glee.

"I'll get saucers to put under the pots so that we don't leave water marks," she promised. "And a little watering can."

The men just nodded and went on with their work.

She developed a routine, one more added to the layers in their department. At exactly eleven thirty on Tuesday and Friday she took the small watering can to the ladies restroom and filled it. On Tuesday she immediately watered the plants, but on Friday she put the watering can on her desk first. She had purchased a plastic caddy at the hardware store and she used it to rotate the plants. First she went to the windowsill and loaded the three right hand plants into the caddy, moved the other two plants to the right, and then went to each of their desks and switched out the plants, returning the three 'used' plants to the saucers on the windowsill. Then she watered all of them. She never varied the steps, and, as with most routines, over time it became just a part of a landscape that never changed.

Of course her goal had been to get near the jacket, and that was working out nicely. On Friday morning of the ninth month, after the trip to vault, she set about working with the plants in the usual way. Her heart was in her throat as she began moving the pots, picking up the first three on the windowsill and shifting the other two, and she was so nervous that she moved away before she remembered that she at least wanted to feel the coat. When she came back with the watering can, she did better. Being naturally left handed, her right hand was free to explore, and she felt something solid in the pocket through the material. She finished watering, put away the caddy and watering can and sat down at her desk. Her face felt flushed, but no one seemed to notice.

At noon Tom Woods stood up, getting ready to go have lunch. "Have a safe trip George. We'll see you on Monday, of course."

"Yes, thank you. Monday at eight sharp."

Then Tom turned to Mildred. "I'm just going out for a sandwich. Can I bring you anything Miss Alcott?"

"Oh, no thank you. I have my lunch right here." She opened the desk drawer, which contained her lunch bag, to show that she meant it. She always ate at her desk to save money, but today it was because she felt weak in the knees.

At twelve thirty, exactly, Mr. Cravetz stood up and put on his jacket and she noticed that he patted his left pocket.

"I'm on my way to lunch, Miss Alcott, and then I'll pick up the briefcase from security and leave for the airport. So I'll just say good-by for the weekend."

"Have a safe trip, Mr. Cravetz," she echoed Mr. Woods.

"Oh yes...thank you." He opened the door and was gone.

Mildred finally took a deep breath. What should she do? Should she do anything? She didn't really know what was in his pocket, after all. It could even be something he had in there all along. So she shouldn't do anything, at least until she knew one way or another if it was one of the gold bars. If it was, she could deal with it then. But she couldn't stop thinking about it. If he was taking a bar, how did he do it? The number of bars always counted out the same, three hundred. They were in neat stacks and rows, six across, five deep, and ten in a stack. She realized that he must be substituting a fake bar. Where would you get something like that? She took out the phone book and looked in the yellow pages under 'gold.' There were a number of listings, mostly for buying and selling gold jewelry, but there were a few that offered imitation gold coins and bars. That had to be it.

The door opened and Tom Woods returned from lunch. "George left?" he said asking the obvious. Then he noticed that she hadn't opened her lunch. "What, not hungry today?"

Mildred closed the phonebook and looked at her lunch bag. "You know what, Mr. Woods? I think I need some fresh air. If you don't mind I'll go out to the courtyard to eat."

"No I don't mind. I think that's a great idea. It's not good to stay in the air-conditioning all day. Go get some sun."

She stepped out of the dark interior of the casino into the bright desert light and had to take a minute to let her eyes adjust. Then she found an empty bench near one of the many fountains and opened her lunch. Maybe she was making a mountain out of a molehill, but what if she wasn't? What if he actually was stealing the gold? She should tell someone, but who would that be? Mr. Woods? The security guard? She tried to imagine Mr. Cravetz in prison and it seemed sad, like putting a mouse into a cage full of alley cats. She had to find out what exactly was in his pocket. She finished her lunch and went back to the office.

She continued to water the plants and rotate them from desk to windowsill, the plants seemed to thrive with that routine, and Mildred began practicing slipping her right hand into the coat pocket as she watered the last plant on the windowsill which put her immediately next to the coat tree. It was a matter of a few seconds, in and out.

Precisely at two minutes to ten on the Friday morning of the tenth month, Mr. Cravetz stood up, retrieved his jacket and made his usual announcement, "Miss Alcott, it's time to go."

"Yes, Mr. Cravetz, I'm ready."

All went as usual and they were back in the office by eleven. At eleven thirty she commenced her routine. By this time neither Mr. Cravetz nor Mr. Woods paid any attention to her as she dealt with the plants, and the process of slipping her hand into his pocket went smoothly, as usual. What wasn't usual was her mental reaction to the touch of the cool metal bar. Now what?

When she hadn't been sure that he was actually taking the gold, the money amount was an abstraction. She had no idea what gold cost. She tried looking in the financial section of the newspaper for information, but found it confusing. She had begun eating her lunch outside on Fridays and she noticed the office of a financial institution located across the street from the casino. Maybe they could tell her. When she opened the door and stepped into the reception area she immediately felt out of place.

"Can I help you?" The smartly dressed young woman made Mildred painfully aware of her own bargain store outfit and sensible shoes.

"Yes...well, I just have a question." She considered turning around and leaving.

"Of course. If you can just tell me the nature of your question, I can have one of our brokers help you."

A broker. This had been a mistake. "That's ok. I just wanted to ask about the cost of gold. I don't know how to look it up." She could feel her face flushing.

"I might be able to help you with that." The young woman looked over to a wall where numbers and charts were flashing around as if it were a theatre marquee. "You can check market prices on the big board. Let's see if I can get you a quote for gold."

Mildred relaxed a little. The young lady was nice.

"There it is." She seemed to have found something to focus on in all of the constantly changing numbers. "Two eighty five. It's in green so that means its up on the day at this point."

"Two eighty five?"

"Yes, two hundred and eight five dollars...that's now. It could change, of course, but probably not by much. Does that answer your question?"

"Yes, that's just what I wanted to know, thank you." She started to leave, but turned back. "I'm sorry, I really don't know anything about gold...what does that price mean?"

"It's the price of gold per ounce."

"Oh, ok, per ounce. Thank you.'

"You're welcome. Anytime." She smiled at Mildred and seemed not to care what she was wearing.

The one extravagance that Mildred had allowed herself was the purchase of a bicycle. It took a number of months to save up, but it had been worth it. As far as she could see, she would never own a car, so this gave her some mobility, a way to get out of her apartment on weekends and get out into the countryside. She had come to appreciate the starkness of the desert around Las Vegas, but this Saturday morning her destination was the Public

Library. She didn't know the conversion rate of ounces to kilograms, well not exactly. She knew it was a lot. Someone in the office probably knew but she didn't want to stir up any curiosity with the question. She locked her bike in the rack and went in.

A slightly harried looking woman behind the checkout desk was fussing with a computer and didn't notice Mildred at first.

"Excuse me."

The woman looked up. "Oh I'm sorry...this machine is giving me fits. I can't get it to power up, or whatever it's called." She gave it a few more jabs without result. "How can I help you?"

"Well, I think I'm looking for a math book. I wanted to look up the conversion rates for inches and pounds to the metric system. Do you know where I'd find that information?"

"I'm sure we have that on the shelf, but if you don't need to read a lot about it...you know, you just want the conversion rates, then I have a little chart right here in the desk." She rifled through a drawer and handed it to Mildred. "Will this do?"

"Yes. It's perfect. Just what I wanted."

"I can make a copy if you like."

"Yes please. That would be great." She'd seen the number she was looking for but thought it would look better if she took a copy of the whole chart.

While the woman, who was obviously technologically challenged, struggled with the copy machine, Mildred did some mental math. *Two hundred eighty five times thirty-five... round up? Down? Make it three hundred times thirty. Good heavens! That's nine thousand!*

The librarian handed her the copy and smiled. "I have to charge for this, twenty-five cents. I should have told you before I made it."

"No, that's fine." Mildred dug into the small pack she wore when she biked, came up with the quarter, and then folded the paper and stuffed it in. "This is just what I needed. Thanks."

Outside she stood for a moment grappling with the enormity of the situation. When she first realized that two hundred eighty five dollars was the price of an ounce, not the kilo bar, she knew this could get out of hand. Now that she had absolute confirmation of the amount of money involved, she had to think. She climbed on her bike and began to ride, first the bike lanes, and then the paths that led to the wide-open spaces outside the city limits.

When she found out that a kilo bar didn't actually weigh thirty-five ounces, it weighed 1000 grams, which was 32.15 ounces, making her original calculations about the bar's worth off by a little more than eight hundred dollars, it didn't matter. It was still a lot of money. She had no idea how long Mr. Cravetz had been at this, but in just the ten months that she had been on the job he had pocketed, literally, more than eighty-two thousand dollars. He had been head of the department for five or six years before she came, and he was so smooth at the switch, that he must have been doing this for at least two or three years already. Again, she struggled with what to do. But after a lot of pedaling, and many evenings spent sitting on her small balcony watching the sun go down, she decided that maybe it wasn't any of her business after all. What was the security guard's responsibility in all of this? It seemed like that was his job, not hers. She would just put it out of her mind.

When she awoke from a dead sleep in the middle of the night a few weeks after the tenth trip to the vault with an outrageously audacious idea, she knew that none of this had ever left her mind. What if *she* switched the bar in Mr. Cravetz' pocket for a fake?

How crazy was that? She couldn't contain herself. She got up, put on her robe, and began pacing through the apartment. "It's times like this I wish I smoked!" The sound of her voice in the empty apartment made her laugh. She went into the kitchen and flipped on the light. *This is just too bizarre!* She pulled the milk and peanut butter from the refrigerator and got a box of crackers from the cabinet. *Could I really do it? I got in and out of his pocket a number of times and he didn't notice.* She sat down at the kitchen table and poured a glass of milk, and then jumped up and found a notepad and pencil. *What do I need? I'll make a list.*

The list was surprisingly short, and, when she felt satisfied that she had thought of everything, she went back to bed. In the morning, in the cold light of day, she took another look at the list while her coffee was brewing. It was simple, nothing difficult to accomplish and it made her feel curiously calm about the whole idea. She really only needed two things: imitation kilo bars, of course, and a pocket of her own. Oh yes, and a lot of nerve. She left the list on the kitchen table and got dressed for work.

She spent the day in the office waiting for the end of it. Her mind was racing with all kinds of ideas, and she was anxious to get home. She picked up a salad and a small bottle of wine - this called for wine - at a supermarket near her home, and settled in to do some serious planning. She would solve the imitation bar acquisition through the yellow pages. She had seen enough ads to make her think they were readily available. After all, Mr. Cravetz got his someplace. As far as the pocket for herself, she could see an easy solution to that. She was always cold in the air-conditioned office, and usually brought a sweater. She would get one with pockets. What she needed to do now was make a list of the pros and cons.

On the pro side, she didn't have to create a plan. It was already in place. The established plant routine allowed her to circulate behind Mr. Cravetz' desk without any suspicion. In fact, the only thing that would actually cause either man to notice her was if she didn't tend to the plants. As far as taking the gold from the vault, that was on Mr. Cravetz, and it certainly looked like she could count on him to hold up that end of the deal. Another plus, a big plus, was the money. As things stood now, her financial future looked bleak. Just one of the kilo bars would bring more money than she could save in years.

The positive side of this idea looked pretty solid. What could go wrong? That's what she needed to consider. The most obvious downside was Mr. Cravetz catching her. But what could he do about it? He couldn't turn her in without incriminating himself. If he wasn't such a quiet, timid little man, she might worry that he could get physical, but that wasn't likely, and, again it would bring attention to him. Of course the worst-case scenario was that they both went to jail, so she would have to take care to protect Mr. Cravetz as he went about his part of the scheme.

Chapter 21

As the years went by everything settled into a comfortable routine, that thing they were best at in their world of accounting. 'Ducks in a row,' Mr. Cravetz was often heard to say. It wasn't until a year had passed, though, that Mildred actually began to relax and believe that her plan was working out. She began to think of it as a partnership with Mr. Cravetz – they were partners in crime and she was the silent one. She saw her part in the actual criminal activity as less serious than that of Mr. Cravetz. After all, she was just taking an already stolen bar. What was that called? Aiding and abetting?

What never ceased to amaze her was that Mr. Cravetz didn't noticed the switch. She had certainly gone out of her way to find the finest imitation bar available, and there were all grades to be had, from gag gift quality to almost jewelry grade and she bought the best. After all, at $10.95 apiece, the discount price when you bought in bulk, it was a solid investment. If he did notice that the bars were imitation, it didn't seem to matter to him because he kept on with his end of the plan. She finally decided that he was so fixated on his own switch and get-away operation that the possibility that he was the target of the same scheme never occurred to him.

She decided early on that she needed to educate herself about money, so she enrolled in a night class called Personal Finance at a nearby junior college. While it was a basic class, it opened her eyes to a world that, up until now, had little meaning for her. Her personal finance activities had consisted of depositing her paycheck, paying her rent, and parceling out enough money to pay for groceries and incidentals for the month. Her savings account amounted to what little she could stick into the proverbial cookie jar to buy a few luxuries, the bicycle being the main one. That was it. Now things were different. She was amassing a sizeable nest egg in a very short time and she needed more sophisticated information.

She became a regular at the library but was careful not to just check out financial books. She knew the librarian, ditzy though she was, took a keen interest in what people read. She mixed it up with historical novels, mysteries, cookbooks, gardening tomes and once a book on crocheting. She felt that she gave the solid appearance of an eclectic reader. She also used the computers at the library. She was saving for one of her own, but it would take awhile since she was in the peculiar situation of being fairly rich but cash poor. In the meantime, the library had installed the latest technology for general use and she discovered that the burgeoning world of the Internet was an amazing font of information. She found that she could subscribe to financial services and receive monthly newsletters that began to fill in her information gap in the world of money.

One thing she needed to know was how to sell the gold. She couldn't just keep stashing the bars in the scrub bucket under the sink, and she could use a little cash. The problem, if it could be considered one, was that even selling one bar meant she would have a lot of cash on hand, and that didn't seem at all safe. Or, more likely, the sale might result in the buyer issuing a check, which would need to be cashed. She had the bank account where she deposited her paycheck each month, but after she wrote checks on it to pay her bills, the balance that was left was only the minimum amount needed to keep from being charged a fee. If she suddenly deposited a large amount of money it might raise suspicions. The bars would have to stay in the bucket for the time being until she figured this out.

That's when she chanced upon the article about discovering your roots. It was immediately clear to her that what she needed to do was take back her maiden name and use it to become an Irish citizen. She wouldn't change her name from Alcott at work, or anyplace in her daily life, just on her new bank account. Mildred O'Malley had a nice ring to it. The process took almost a year, and by the time she was able to establish another account she had amassed twenty-nine bars...heavy bars. She had paid for a safety deposit box, but she quickly realized that she couldn't put them all in one box, even though they would fit, because the bank employee who brought out the box would certainly notice the heft of it and wonder about the contents. So she opened accounts at several other banks and spread her wealth around.

By this time she had figured out how to sell the gold. She found any number of companies dealing in precious metals through the Internet and it turned out to be a simple process. All it took was a call to a dealer to get a guaranteed quote on the amount she wanted to sell, and then ship it. The dealer recommended sending it registered mail through the Post Office, and that's what she did with the first bar, but it made her very uneasy to have to declare a value to get the insurance, especially since it was going to the address of a precious metals firm. Maybe she looked like she might have something worth nine thousand dollars to sell, the family jewelry perhaps, but she couldn't do this again. At some point she needed to sell multiple bars and she certainly didn't look like a person with that kind of money. Even if the post office employees paid little attention to the mailing, there were other customers standing within hearing distance and the possibility of it being someone from work made it too nerve wracking for her. This shipping process required more thought.

Armored car delivery seemed a better option, but there was hitch, of course. The bar had to be shipped the same day the quote was given, which was doable through the Post Office because she could go on Saturday morning. But the delivery services had nine to five hours during the week and were closed on the weekend. She couldn't manage it without time off from work, and she wouldn't do that. That would cause talk. Even the tomato in payroll would notice and probably make a big deal of it. She would have to use her vacation time.

Chapter 22

The subject of vacation schedules had come up, along with benefit packages, shortly after she first arrived.

"Miss Alcott, have you thought about vacation time for yourself?" Mr. Woods had asked.

"No, not really." She was focused on being at work, any work, so that time off hadn't occurred to her.

"Well, it's early yet. But, you can have a one-week vacation toward the end of your first year, and then after that you're entitled to two weeks a year. I thought you might want to start making some plans." He produced a calendar from his desk drawer." Mr. Cravetz and I have marked out our time here, so you'll want to work around us. We don't like to have two people out at a time." He handed her the calendar.

She looked at the weeks and months that stretched out before she could mark a spot, but was really just glad that she might think about being here for that long. As far as a vacation, she had nowhere to go. If she was thrifty she could possible save up enough to take in a movie or two at matinee prices during a week at home. She finally chose a week at random and then noticed that Mr. Cravetz was marked for just one week so far.

"I hope I'm not choosing a week that you want, Mr. Cravetz." The sound of her voice caused him to look in her general direction.

"I beg your pardon?"

"I'm just looking at the vacation schedule and I see Mr. Woods has two weeks blocked out, but I only see one for you." She felt reckless addressing such a personal topic to him. "I'm wondering if the week I'm picking might be one that you..." she trailed off.

"Don't worry, Miss Alcott. I only take one week." He paused for a moment and then launched into the longest conversation...well not a conversation since that implies a back and forth exchange of ideas...but statement since she had been here. "I go camping in the desert every year. I quite like the desert and it's flora and fauna, although some people find it monotonous. I find it quite varied." He reached into his desk drawer and produced a pad of some sort. "I like to sketch the terrain and its denizens." He actually got up and came over to her desk and presented her with what turned out to be a sketchbook.

She turned the pages and was impressed with the artistic quality of the works. "These drawings are very good, Mr. Cravetz." She could feel him beaming. "You should get them framed."

"It's enough to have the book." He took it back from her and returned to his desk. She imagined he was quite exhausted from the effort he had just exerted.

Later in the day, when he was out for lunch, her tomato acquaintance stopped by her desk. "I heard Mr. Cravetz telling you about his annual trip to the desert."

"Yes, he showed me the sketches that he'd made. They are really quite good." She wanted to beat the negative remark that she knew was coming.

"Yeah, he shows them around the office every year. He's not bad. And he always invites the guys in the office to go camping with him, too." Here it came. "But no one wants to spend a whole week, *alone,* with Mr. Personality. Can you imagine it? And even if they did, he always goes in September...the hottest time of the year around here." She shook her head. "What's he thinking?"

"Well, its nice of him to ask, I'm sure." She picked up a stack of papers and began to shuffle them around hoping to indicate that she was going back to work. Miss Tomato, who looked more like Miss Eggplant in a purple outfit today, got the hint and moved on.

Mildred looked at the two weeks she had marked off for vacation this year and immediately saw a problem. One of the weeks was the last week of the month. She couldn't be away. She would change it tomorrow. The other week was scheduled in three months. She would use that week to sell another bar, well maybe two.

She spoke to Mr. Woods right away when she got to work. "I think I want to change my vacation time, if that's possible."

"I don't see why not." He pulled the schedule from his desk and handed it to her. "It doesn't really matter. Well, I should say, it doesn't matter if it's not tax time."

"I'm not thinking of changing to another week." He looked puzzled. "I'm wondering what would happen if I only took one week? I notice that's what Mr. Cravetz does."

"I've never asked about that. You're right about George, though. Let me call Personnel." He got the answer right away. "They said that you can't bank the time to take an extended vacation, but it could accrue to your retirement date...you could retire earlier. Does that idea interest you?"

"Yes." She found that she didn't want to be away from the office anymore than necessary because she wanted to keep an eye on Mr. Cravetz. She would like to arrange her vacation for the same week that he was gone, but that wasn't possible, so she would take one week early in the month and take care of shipping and banking.

The armored car service turned out to be the answer. They were used to shipping large amounts of cash and securities and bullion, so they thought nothing of her transactions. It was all handled by appointment under armed security and all you needed was the money to pay for the shipping and your ID. She used her Irish passport.

It was in 2002 that she got a pleasant surprise when she called the dealer to get a quote for the fifth bar that she planned to sell. She was offered more this year. The price for the previous bars had hovered around nine thousand dollars apiece. This year the quote was eleven thousand dollars and some change. She'd gotten a raise! With this year's check she would have around forty-five thousand dollars spread around three banks, and, up to this point, it was all in checking accounts. That wasn't smart. It should be earning some interest. She spent the last day of her vacation, depositing the latest check, and moving much of the money in each of the three banks into savings accounts. She felt better now.

But the thing of it was, the forty-five thousand was only the cash in the bank. She had twenty-eight bars stored in safety deposit boxes, and, at the price quoted this year, that was over three hundred thousand dollars...not earning interest. She guessed she could sell the gold and put it into savings, but that seemed like a bad plan. Once again she thought she would attract attention to herself with large deposits at the banks. She could invest in stocks perhaps, but how? She couldn't go into a brokerage house because it presented the same problem as shipping gold from the post office, someone from work might recognize her. She had been careful to cultivate an image of someone living from paycheck to paycheck. Her clothes were inexpensive, not to say cheap, and her personal appearance ran to

the dowdy side. She kept her hair long - haircuts cost money –
and she began to pull it back into a bun. She chose wire rims for
her glasses, wore no jewelry, and the only makeup she allowed
herself was a slight dab of lipstick.

A personal stockbroker was out of the question. It *was*
possible to invest through the Internet, but she knew nothing
about investing. She would have to do something about that. She
had always been good at math, which led to the bookkeeping job,
but she didn't have the money to go to college, let alone think
about *investing* money, so she had much to learn. She set about
her self-education program with a zeal inspired by her growing
wealth. During the next two years the price of gold continue to
move higher, not by a lot, but enough to keep her focused on the
future. She decided not to sell any more bars until she had a
better plan. Right now just holding the gold was earning money.

By the end of 2004 she had approximately sixty-five kilo bars
worth close to a million dollars, and she was considerably more
informed about markets and investments, in fact, so
knowledgeable that she hesitated to do anything. The stock
market was in a decline and real estate was edgy. For every
positive narrative about investing in either venue, there was a
negative one to balance it out. She finally decided that the best
course of action for her was to do nothing...for now...and keep
stockpiling the bars.

The weight of the bars was another problem. She had safety
deposit boxes in three banks, two of which allowed her to retrieve
her own box and open it in a private room. The third bank
required the assistance of a teller to access the box. In the
beginning, when she only had twenty-five bars, she had spread
them evenly among the three boxes, which meant each box
weighed approximately sixteen pounds. But she was put on her
guard when she went to the bank to put in two more bars.

"Lady, what have you got in here?" The vault teller slid the
box across the counter. "...lead weights?" He made the remark in

a joking way, but it made Mildred think twice about adding more weight. She decided to take two bars out instead. Then, when she added four bars to one of the boxes in another bank, she could see that this wasn't going to work. The box now weighed forty pounds and she struggled to lift it without showing any visible strain. The idea of opening more bank accounts to get access to storage seemed non-productive. She needed another storage option.

Chapter 23

On one of her regular weekend biking outings she noticed a building that she had passed dozens of times – a public storage facility. She wheeled into the parking lot and was happy to see that the office was open. She leaned her bike against the side of the building and went in.

"Good morning." Her greeting caused the plus-sized woman behind the desk to put down the newspaper and stand up.

"Can I help you?"

"I'm thinking of renting storage space...I'm wondering what it costs."

"Depends on the size you need." She pushed a chart across the counter and pointed to the prices. "The smallest unit we got is five by five...it's twenty-three dollars a month...first month's just a dollar though. Then they go up to five by ten, and that runs you thirty-nine a month. Still get first month for a dollar." She looked at Mildred expectantly.

"You obviously mean feet."

Mildred's comment brought on paroxysms of laughter. When the woman could catch her breath she wheezed, "Wouldn't that be something! What if it was inches?" and she was off again.

When the woman finally composed herself, Mildred asked, "Could I see one of the small units?"

"You bet, honey." She plucked a key off of a board behind the desk. "Unit two...it's right close by." She lumbered from behind the counter and led the way out of the office down a sidewalk to one of several doors spread out down the length of the building.

"So how does this work?" Mildred was trailing behind.

"Well, it's pretty easy." She pointed to the other doors on the outside. "All them doors lead into the same kind of hallway as this one here." She pulled open the door and they stepped inside. Mildred could see that there were locker doors running down the wide corridor, maybe eight or ten on either side. The woman unlocked unit two. "All these doors have a regular lock, and you can just use that, but we recommend you get yourself a combination lock." She pointed to the lock hasp on the doorjamb. "We sell 'em in the office if you don't have one already."

Mildred stepped into what was essentially a box...five feet by five feet by...she looked up.

"Ceiling's ten feet, honey. You can get some sizable furniture in here...and it's climate controlled." She seemed to think that was a deal maker.

"Oh, that's good...climate controlled."

"You can store your furniture, your art work...whatever you got without worrying about 'em. They won't mildew or buckle."

"That's good."

"Everything's secure. We got cameras here in the hall...and these here hallways is always lighted." She had stepped back out of the storage unit to point out the security features. "You got a lot to store, honey?"

"Not too much...I live in an apartment but I don't have any storage there...to speak of."

"Oh lord, I know how that is. I have a little two bedroom place myself and I've just about filled up one of them with all my extras...I like to buy the big economy size stuff, toilet paper and the like...saves me a bundle. But then where do you put it?"

"Yes, that's right," Mildred sympathized. "It can get tight."

They were back outside by now and the woman pointed to a number of security cameras around the parking lot. "We got these cameras going night and day...and you can put stuff in your unit twenty-four seven if you like." She lowered her voice. "But, honey, I don't recommend females coming around after dark. You know...it's not smart. That's just what I think."

"Oh no. I think you're right about that. I'd only be coming during the day." By this time they were back in the office. "I'd like to rent the small unit. I don't have my checkbook with me, but I can come back later."

"You got a dollar?"

"Yes."

"Then you can fill out the paper work and pay for the first month...remember?...just a dollar, and then you're all signed up. Pay for the next month when you come back to put stuff in."

"Ok." She took the forms that she was offered and looked them over. The questions weren't intrusive, just name and address and phone number.

"Now if you get behind on your monthly payments, we notify you and give you a chance to catch up. But if we don't hear from you after three months...we think that's fair...then we can confiscate what's in the unit and sell it to pay your arrears." She was underlining a paragraph in the agreement for Mildred's benefit. "We recommend you pay a year in advance so's not to have that happen."

"That's a good idea." By this time Mildred had signed the agreement and handed over her dollar. The woman tore off the top sheet and handed it to her.

"Glad to have you here, honey."

"Thanks." Mildred took the key to unit two and put it in her pocket.

She rented the storage unit under the name Mildred Alcott, so there would be no connection to the banks. She could see that she needed to actually store a few pieces of furniture because it would look odd to the woman if she didn't put anything more than a box in there, and she was pretty sure that she kept an eye on what went on. Mildred had noticed the security monitor behind the desk when she was signing the papers. It showed split screen displays of the parking lot and the hallways.

She didn't have extra furniture to spare in her apartment that she could put in storage, but she knew of a rundown market street nearby with antique shops, second-hand stores, and pawnshops. She biked that way. The second-hand stores turned out to be pricier than one of the antique establishments where she found several bargains – a small chest, badly in need of paint, a wobbly kitchen chair, and a painting of the desert in a cracked wooden frame. In all, it cost her forty-nine dollars. She had to have the pieces put on hold so that she could come back with her checkbook...and a car, and she knew where she could get that. Two blocks from her apartment was a car rental company. She took her bike back to the apartment, got her checkbook and walked the two blocks. She was able to rent a small van for the day, pick up her new storage furniture, store it in the locker, pay for the year, and return the car by three in the afternoon. By the time she was finally home, she was worn out but exhilarated! She had accomplished a lot in one day. Tomorrow she would take some of the bars to the locker. Right now she was going to cook a small steak and have a nice glass of red wine.

Chapter 24

By 2006 the price of gold had continued to move up, closing at $635.70 at year's end. That made her worth almost two million dollars. This was getting out of hand, and it made sense to stop while she was ahead, but she'd come to enjoy the game. It was rather addictive, actually. There was an obvious ending point...when Mr. Cravetz stopped, which would happen when the real kilo bars ran out or, worst-case scenario, when he was found out. But even if that happened, her position seemed secure. And at this point in her life, she didn't have anything else to pull her away. Maybe that was what she needed to address, a plan for her future. Up to now the idea of investing the money had no real goal, except to make more money. What was it she wanted? Well, security for one thing, a chance to see a little of the world for another...those were two goals that she could plan for.

She began to explore the world from her kitchen table on the computer that she had finally invested in. She wanted a home of her own, she wasn't sure where, but she felt like she needed to put plenty of miles between Las Vegas and that home, whenever she left. Ireland was the natural choice, but everything she was reading about Irish property values made her hesitate to invest in anything there. All of the news was of the skyrocketing prices of real estate. But as she looked elsewhere in the world, in places you might want to live, the news was the same. She would be buying at the top of a market. Well, she had time so she would just keep an eye on the prices...and dream a little.

Then in 2008 it happened – the real estate bubble burst! Prices were dropping around the globe, most particularly, from Mildred's point of view, in Ireland. She had spent the past two years reading every financial analysis that she could access. While the price of gold continued to climb, some analysts felt the prices of other investments, such as real estate, were overvalued and gold acted as a hedge against disaster. So when disaster hit, Mildred was ready. By the end of 2007 she had opened a bank account in Ireland...she had been amazed that she could do that over the phone...sold twenty-six bars for a little more than six hundred and ninety thousand dollars, and had the money wired to her Irish account. Then she set about looking for a place to buy, through the Internet, of course.

She was bewildered by the experience. She had no idea what she was looking at and so finally took the chance to contact an estate agent through her Irish bank.

"Oh yes, the Irish real estate market is a force to be dealt with, there's no denying that." The woman was charming. She suggested that perhaps, since Mildred said that she probably wouldn't be moving to Ireland immediately, she find a property that could be used as a rental until that time.

"How would I manage the rental from so far away? I suppose there are agencies..." She hadn't given much thought to the care of a house that she wouldn't inhabit right away.

"Oh, yes, any number of agencies. It's really quite common these days to have absentee owners...and sellers. There's so many that bought in when our prices were going up, thinking it could never end, and hoping for a financial windfall I expect. But I'm afraid their hopes got a bit of a comeuppance instead. It's why you're seeing so many wonderful opportunities come on the market. Why don't I put together a portfolio of properties that might fit your needs and send it off to you?'

"Yes, that would be fine." She gave the woman the post office box number belonging to Mildred O'Malley. She had opened that when she set up the three bank accounts to handle her bank statements and it had been very useful over the years. The O'Malley identity received all of the important mail, payment checks from gold dealers – she did business with more than one, as a precaution – monthly financial newsletters, and now a real estate *portfolio.* She was evolving, she hoped, from prospective pensioner to moneyed property owner.

A note in her P.O. box announced the arrival of the portfolio and she had to pick up the oversized package at the counter. She could hardly wait to get home to begin to look at her future. There were fifteen different properties, all interesting, but two stood out. The first was a 'traditional' Irish cottage, with a thatched roof even, but modern improvements throughout. The second was much more imposing, and expensive...a Georgian style country home that was presently being used as a B&B. It was several kilometers outside of a small village on acreage that was rented out to a neighbor as pastureland for their dairy cows. A middle-aged couple managed the bed and breakfast business, and they hoped to continue their employment with a new owner. The estate agent said both of these properties were easy to rent and would bring in income, the B&B had bookings through the year, and income from the land, and the cottage was always popular with vacationers. Mildred chose the expensive one.

For the first time in her life, Mildred felt a sense of security. She found great comfort in owning land, even land she had never seen. This would be her investment plan then. She began looking at homes in other countries. Why not?...she had the money. The price of gold had been rising, but now it began a surge that had the world taking notice. By the middle of 2010 the price had increased 30% over the previous year and the one hundred and seven kilo bars that she had stored between the banks and the public storage unit were worth approximately five million dollars. This was crazy! She was fully aware that the market could go south in the blink of an eye and she should sell. She decided on half.

She always took her vacation the first week in August, which was the week that she could handle her banking. This year she was busier than usual. She sold seventeen bars to each of the three dealers that she did business with, on three separate days, loading the bars into a backpack – she could manage the weight - and rode to three different armored car companies and completed the shipments. Maybe she was being over cautious, but she felt better for it. The sale of fifty-one bars netted $2,295,510.

She did the same in August of 2011. This time she sold 30 bars, a little under half of what she had at the time, and made almost a million and a half dollars. The Irish bank account was bursting. Things couldn't keep on this way, although there were long-shot predictions that gold could go to $5,000, but Mildred didn't want to take the chance.

In August of 2012 she sold the remaining bars that she held, fifty, for $1679.50 an ounce - $2,699,796.25. She missed the top of the market, $1896, by one month, but then that wasn't her vacation week.

Chapter 25

After the sale was completed and the money was banked, Mildred decided it was time to retire, not from her bookkeeping job, but her partnership with Mr. Cravetz. Her run of luck had been unbelievable and it seemed to tempt fate to keep going. She would let Mr. Cravetz keep whatever was left of the vault horde. The first month that she didn't switch the bar in his coat pocket she wondered if he would notice, but he didn't. She knew that this whole thing would come to an end sooner than later and she began to think about an exit strategy for herself.

She was a little reluctant to abandon Mr. Cravetz – he had needed her help several times over the years. Twice a new security guard had joined their monthly vault outing and it had been the cause of concern for both Mildred and Mr. Cravetz, although they certainly never discussed their mutual fears. When Henry retired, a new guard was assigned to their team and Mildred could see it rattled Mr. Cravetz. The new man was not as personable as Henry and he looked askance when the gold cart was rolled out.

"What's this?" The guard was clearly confused.

"This is the gold, coins and bars, that is stored in the vault for the convenience of the patrons of the casino." Mildred could hear the nervousness in Mr. Cravetz' voice. "We do an accounting of it each month." He pulled the ledger off of the safe shelf and then began his usual counting of the coins and bars.

Mildred could see that he was unsteady and stepped in to divert the guard's attention. "Mr. Cravetz is meticulous, you know, about this account." The guard looked up at her and she went on. "He always says that you can't be too careful with other people's money...don't you agree?"

"Uh...oh yes, yes I do."

"He's set up a wonderful system and he never varies from it."

"Oh, yes?"

"Yes, that way the casino always knows that this account is in good order...all their ducks are in a row... am I right Mr. Cravetz?"

By this time he had finished the count, and the switch, and was pushing the cart back into the safe.

"Yes, indeed, Miss Alcott. All our ducks are in a row."

This security guard soon fell into the routine and Mr. Cravetz seemed to relax, although Mildred kept a cautious watch each month. When he left after two years, and the third man joined their trio, Mildred was a master at running interference.

There had been another incident in September of 2011, and it had taken quick thinking and a steady head on her part to smooth the situation over. On the last Friday of September, when they made their usual trip to the vault, they were shocked to see that one of the kilo bars was missing from the stack. They had gone through the usual process of entering their separate parts of the combination, but when Mr. Cravetz opened the safe door and reached for the cart, he froze.

This sudden break in the routine, small as it might seem, alerted Mildred. "Mr. Cravetz, what's wrong?"

"The gold," he sounded hoarse. "It's missing!"

"What!" Sam pushed up to the cart. "No, it's here Mr. Cravetz."

"A bar is missing."

By this time, he had rolled the cart out into the room and they could all see what he was talking about. One kilo bar was missing from the stack. It was a small bar, but it left a gaping hole in the golden block. Mildred could see that it had shaken Mr. Cravetz, so much so that he looked dazed.

Sam reached for the phone jacketed on his belt. "I'm going to call the head of security!"

That was last thing that Mildred wanted to happen. It was alarming to think of any outside interest in this affair, and by the looks of Mr. Cravetz, all kinds of unwanted attention would descend on this routine.

"Wait, Sam," she said. "Before you call, let's see if there's an entry in the ledger for the missing gold. There must be an explanation for this."

"All right, Miss Alcott," Sam took his hand off of his phone and reached for the book where these monthly activities were recorded. He put it on the table and looked at Mr. Cravetz. "Do you want to check this, sir?"

George Cravetz looked at the book and then opened it out to the most current page. There, noted on September 23 as the most recent entry, was a receipt for one kilo gold bar, signed by Max Grenwald and William Luntz. They all stared at the entry.

Mildred broke the silence. "Oh good, it's accounted for." She thought that her relief must be obvious, but neither man seemed to notice.

"Mr. Grenwald must have the combination, too," Mr. Cravetz muttered. "I thought it was just me."

Mildred could see that Sam was puzzled by Mr. Cravetz' behavior. She needed to head him off. "Well, this is certainly an unusual event for us! It must have surprised you too, Sam."

The guard nodded and gave a little chuckle. "Sure did. More like a jolt."

By this time Mr. Cravetz had started the inventory of the gold and it looked like he had recovered his composure.

Mildred ventured one more question. "Sam, I know Mr. Grenwald is the manager, but who is William Luntz?"

"He's one of the night security guards. When I saw his name I knew it was ok...the transaction and all. Security was in on it."

Apparently the explanation satisfied Mr. Cravetz because he went on with his usual routine. Mildred could see the usual slight sag in his jacket as he stood gazing at the gold on the cart, hands in his pockets. He didn't seem fazed by this intrusion into their private world of embezzlement.

It was the second week in September of 2013, when Mr. Cravetz didn't return from his vacation, that Mildred knew the end was in sight. That Monday morning, at 8:15, she and Mr. Woods looked at each other and then at Mr. Cravetz' empty desk.

"This is strange," Mr. Woods looked worried. "Where could George be? You don't suppose the clock is wrong, do you?"

Mildred glanced at her watch, but knew that there was no mistake with the time on the clock. "It's not wrong."

"Well...there's a first time for everything, I guess."

They turned back to their work, but Mildred caught Mr. Woods looking up at the clock almost as often as she did. At eleven he took the employee directory out of his desk.

"I'm going to give his house a call...maybe he's sick...." He didn't sound convinced of that. He found the number and dialed, but there was no answer. "Well, that didn't help."

"I don't suppose he has a cell phone?" Mildred ventured. They both knew he didn't.

"No. No cell phone." Tom Woods frowned. "I should have suggested that to him...that he should get a cell phone when he went on vacation...in case something happened, like a flat tire, or..."

"Yes, maybe he's had car trouble." She hesitated, and added, "or he's been in an accident! You don't think that's what happened, do you?"

"Now, Miss Alcott, don't fret about that. I'm sure we would have heard something if that was the case...he has identification."

"Yes. That's right."

Mildred watched as he called Mr. Cravetz' house several more times during the afternoon, always with the same result, no answer. Finally the workday, which had seemed painfully long, was over, and they began gathering up their things to go home.

Mr. Woods cleared his throat and said, "Now, Miss Alcott, don't go home and worry about this. I'm sure he'll be here tomorrow."

"Yes, of course, he'll be here in the morning." She folded up her sweater, put it in the drawer, and gathered up her purse and lunch bag. "I'm just going to put it out of my mind."

"That's good."

Of course, that was the last thing she planned to do.

Chapter 26

She sat at the kitchen table with a glass of wine – she noticed that she'd begun buying more wine when the gold market started to run up – and a folder that contained a signed purchase agreement dated August 10, 2013. The villa was hers. Since she had made the first purchase, her country B&B in Ireland, she had added two more modest Irish rentals to her investment portfolio. It had been a sensible use of her money. But this one, this *villa*, had been a purchase from the heart. She loved it the minute she saw the real estate brochure, flowers tumbling over garden walls, small fountains in various parts of the grounds, and views of the sea from the windows and the terrace. She didn't hesitate for a minute – she bought it. This was where she was going when she left Las Vegas – Grimaud on the Cote d'Azure – Villa Tournesol. It meant sunflower, a symbol of good luck, long life, and happiness – a good omen for her new life.

She needed to make a list of all the things she should take care of before she could make her exit. She had already consolidated the O'Malley bank accounts into one when she sold all of the gold. She didn't need the safety deposit boxes any more, just as she didn't need the public storage unit. She donated the few items that she had accumulated there to the Salvation Army and they came and picked them up. She would have to close Mildred Alcott's bank account, cancel her renters insurance, and...what else? Think of a reason to quit, of course. What if Mr. Cravetz came back tomorrow? She would quit anyway. She was ready to start the next part of her life. Mr. Cravetz would just have to fend for himself.

He didn't come in on Tuesday and at 9:30 Tom Woods called Charles Black, assistant manager of the casino. Mildred could only hear one side of the conversation but it was enough to alarm her.

"Mr. Black thinks you should check the books? Why would he say that?"

Tom Woods shook his head. "I guess he's worried that George took off with company funds."

"Oh, Mr. Cravetz would *never* do anything like that!"

"Well, you and I both know that, but I guess, if you didn't know George like we do, it might look suspicious when someone who's never missed a day of work all of a sudden does...*and* doesn't call in to the office. Mr. Black is just being cautious."

"Well, when he does come back, I hope he doesn't hear about this. I think it would crush him...he bends over backwards to make sure everything is handled in a professional way."

"Yes he does, Miss Alcott. Now don't worry...there's nothing wrong with the books. George always has me double check his figures...he couldn't doctor the books if he wanted to."

It crossed Mildred's mind that he probably could, *if* he wanted to.

Later in the day Charles Black came into the accounting office.

"So, how do they look Tom?" He sat down in the chair next to his desk.

"Everything's in order," answered Tom with a slight shrug of his shoulders. "The man's meticulous. Nothing out of line in his bookwork, and his money delivery to the Midwest is, and always has been faultless."

Mildred listened as the men discussed the possibilities of the misfortunes that could have befallen Mr. Cravetz. Of course something *could* have happened to him if he was camping in the desert, but she didn't think he was. She had decided years ago that was a cover for wherever he really went. When you knew what he was doing with the kilo bars, then his professed camping vacation each year took on an aura of theater. He knew that no one would go with him, but he always asked. And he always brought back the sketchbook and shared it around the office, even in payroll, which was the only time he ever interacted with that department. You couldn't tell where he'd been from the drawings because they were generic desert scenes.

But when Mr. Black suggested that Mr. Cravetz could be dead in his house, Mildred had to consider that possibility. He lived alone, just as she did, and, knowing how reticent he was in the office, probably had no relationship with his neighbors. She and Mr. Woods were the only people who would worry when he didn't show up for work. But, with it being his vacation time, it was an entire week before they could begin to worry. Yes, it was possible that he was dead in his house, and she was relieved when Mr. Black said he would go investigate.

But her relief turned to anxiety just as Mr. Black was about to leave. Mr. Woods informed him that the casino had a gold account and Mr. Cravetz was in charge of it, obviously news to Mr. Black, who said that he wanted to check it out after he went out to the Cravetz house. Mildred calmed herself with the sure knowledge that, even if they did discover the problem with the gold, there was no way to connect her to it. She hoped.

While Mr. Black was out at Mr. Cravetz' house, Mr. Woods called the insurance company to see if they had heard from any medical facilities about a claim.

He shook his head as he hung up. "Nothing, I'm afraid, Miss Alcott." He unlocked his desk drawer and took out the black leather folder that Mr. Cravetz left with him when he went on vacation. It was office protocol...in case the gold had to be accessed for a casino guest. "I'll run this up to Mr. Black's office." He opened it and ran his finger across the rows and down the columns. The folder contained the information about the money transfers and the gold account. "It's all up to date."

"I'm sure it is," said Mildred. "He always makes a record of the vault transactions immediately." She must have sounded defensive, because Mr. Woods gave her a wry smile.

"Of course he does. He's a perfectionist...and as honest as the day is long, to boot." He stood up, folder in hand. "I just wish we would hear something. I'm worried about him."

"So am I...really worried."

When the day was finally over, Mildred was exhausted. Mr. Black had insisted that they handle the gold accounting in the usual manner, which meant counting the coins and the individual kilo bars, and then he said he wanted to take two of the bars with him. Of course he could do that, he's the boss, but why would he if he didn't suspect something. This was *certainly* the end for Mr. Cravetz' plan. She hoped he wasn't coming back, because she could see prison looming in his future. She wanted to go soon. She was ready...she just needed an opportunity to arise that wouldn't set off alarms in peoples' minds.

On Thursday afternoon Mr. Black checked both kilo bars back into the vault, but he didn't say anything about them, one way or another. Mildred wasn't sure what to think. Maybe he was waiting to confront Mr. Cravetz, but he was still missing.

Then on Friday things got worse. Mr. Grenwald showed up in accounting asking about Mr. Cravetz and the cash delivery to

Kansas City, which was due to go out that day. He said Mr. Black was out of town and he would just have to make the delivery himself. Of course that meant another trip to the vault and another accounting of the gold. Mildred couldn't tell if he thought anything was wrong with the gold bars, but he was certainly put out by the idea of counting all of them individually. Why do that, he wondered, when you could see what was there. *Why indeed,* Mildred thought

On Saturday morning she biked over to the public storage company once more. This time she rented the large unit and paid for the year. She would need this space soon. When she left Las Vegas she planned to put all of the furniture in her apartment into storage and let it be sold, after the year went by, to cover her *arrears.*

Monday morning a delivery service presented Mr. Woods with an envelope from an auto impound yard containing a notice that they had towed Mr. Cravetz' car. It was considered abandoned in an airport parking lot. This created all kinds of commotion in the office. By this time the people in payroll knew that George Cravetz was missing, and the theories were flying around..."he was dead in the desert," "someone killed him and stole his car," or "he took that cash delivery he was in charge of and took off for parts unknown." Mildred pointed out that Mr. Grenwald made the delivery this month, and then she got quite emotional, which was a surprise to her, and caused Angie from payroll to apologize.

"Oh honey, I didn't mean to make you cry!" She looked genuinely contrite. "We shouldn't be joking around about something like this. He could be laid out dead, and here we are, laughing."

We're not all laughing, thought Mildred, but said, "We're just so worried." She looked at Mr. Woods. "What should we do about the car?"

"I'm going to take this to Mr. Black." He stood up and picked up the impound notice. "I think we should call the police, but I guess I should check with him first."

Two detectives from the Missing Persons division asked questions around the accounting and payroll departments and management, but came up with nothing. They sent a patrol car to George Cravetz' house, forced open a door and found the same thing, nothing. Only one set of fingerprints turned up on his car and they belonged to him, although that didn't rule out the possibility that a car thief wore gloves. No airline tickets had been purchased in his name since his vacation began, and there was no lead to follow about where he could have gone camping. By the end of the week the case was put into the 'unsolved' file.

The following week the buzz around the office was that Mr. Grenwald was retiring. Angie delivered that news.

"Personnel told us. They want us to set up the books for the new man coming in...some bigwig from Atlantic City."

Mildred felt really uneasy about this development. New management probably meant a review of the books, which proved to be the case.

Tom Woods returned from Mr. Black's office and confided in Mildred in a very hushed voice, "Mr. Black said an outside firm will be doing an audit, but we shouldn't mention anything about the gold account."

Mildred didn't know whether to be alarmed or relieved. "Why not?"

"He said it's never been reported and he didn't want to stir up questions about it. He said the new man in charge agrees with him."

"Well, *I* certainly won't mention it." It struck her as odd that Mr. Black seemed to be protecting the gold, but that worked in her favor. "When will the auditors come?"

"Not for another month, as I understand it." He hesitated. "Another thing he told me is that we are getting a new boss since it looks like George is really gone."

"It won't be you?" Mildred knew he must be sorely disappointed by this news. After all the years he'd put in, it seemed natural for him to move up.

"No. Not me. Mr. Barcone is bringing in his head bookkeeper from the Atlantic City casino. It's closing, you know."

"That seems so unfair!" Mildred really felt bad for him.

Mr. Woods just nodded. "I have to admit, I was sort of counting on it...after it looked like George wouldn't be coming back. But this other man was about to be out of a job altogether."

"It's still not right."

"Thanks, Miss Alcott. I'll just have to make the best of it."

Angie brought the news again. "Have ya heard the latest?" She didn't wait for an answer. "They're giving early retirement packages."

"Who is?" asked Tom Woods.

"The management...here! So, wadda ya think, Mr. Woods? You got enough years to retire early?"

"I doubt it Angie. I can't retire now, anyway. I've got kids ready to start college."

"What about you Miss Alcott? You look like the right age. Maybe you can qualify."

Nobody ever accused you of too much tactfulness, Angie. But Mildred knew that she looked older than she really was. Over the years her hair had turned prematurely white, her Irish genes she supposed, and she had continued to cultivate her spinster look. Well, that hadn't been hard. She had maintained the lifestyle of a person with a bookkeepers' salary, which would preclude trips to the beauty shop, or a more fashionable wardrobe.

"I don't think so. I haven't been here long enough."

"What about all these years of only taking one week vacation?" Mr. Woods asked. "Maybe that will help...that is if you want to retire."

"I've been thinking about it, Mr. Woods." Mildred saw a marvelous opportunity opening up in front of her, a chance to leave without raising eyebrows. "It's not the same without Mr. Cravetz and I'm not sure I can start all over with a new boss. It would be different if that was you, but..." She shook her head. "I just don't know."

Mildred was the first person called in for a review. Angie, who was spending a lot more time at their end of the office now that Mr. Cravetz was gone, said they were going in alphabetical order.

Mr. Black stood up when she came into the conference room. "Come in, Miss Alcott, have a seat." He sat back down, picked up a folder from the stack in front of him, and nodded toward the woman seated at the table. "This is Mrs. Anderson from personnel."

"How do you do?" Mildred inquired, a little nervously.

"I don't know if you've heard" Mr. Black went on, "but we are looking into offering early retirement to a number of individuals."

"I did hear something like that." Mildred answered.

"Yes, well we want to begin to trim expenses here at the casino and one of those ways is to reduce personnel through retirement, early retirement in some cases."

"Yes sir."

"Mr. Black seems to think you might qualify." Mrs. Anderson looked doubtful. "But I see that you've only been here sixteen years." Mr. Black had handed the folder to the woman and she was peering into it. "Your age might be a problem, too." She handed the folder back to Charles Black. "She's just forty-eight, Mr. Black."

"Yes, that's a little on the young side, but I saw a note in the file, Mrs. Anderson, that she only takes one week of vacation a year so that she might put those other weeks toward an earlier retirement date."

"That's right, Mr. Black," Mildred offered. "Mr. Woods asked the personnel department about that when I first started working here and they said that was possible."

"I'm sure they were thinking three or four *months* early," Mrs. Anderson looked skeptical, "not fourteen years."

"Let me ask you a question, Miss Alcott." Mr. Black ignored the woman's observation, "if it *was* possible to retire now, would you want to?"

"Yes...I think I'd like that. With Mr. Cravetz gone, I don't look forward to the day like I used to." She held her breath. She'd already decided if she didn't qualify for this package she would quit anyway. This was helping her lay the foundation for that move. But, to her surprise, Mr. Black came to her defense.

"You've been through a lot, Miss Alcott, in your department." He ignored the quizzical look from the woman. "I'm looking at your performance reviews, which have always been excellent, and coupled with the forfeiture of your vacation time, I think we could work out a nice plan for you." By this time the woman was staring at him. "Let's face it Mrs. Anderson. If Miss Alcott would like to take advantage of the package, it means that we won't be faced with laying someone else off. I know Mr. Barcone wouldn't like that."

"Well...if you think that's best."

"I do. Now, let's see if we can structure a payment plan."

Mildred realized that she'd been holding her breath. There was a surreal quality to this whole affair – she wanted to leave, but she really didn't qualify, and then Mr. Black steps in and makes it happen.

"Mr. Black...I don't know what to say. Thank you."

"You're welcome, Miss Alcott. As I said, you've been through a lot with George's disappearance. Management certainly appreciates your commitment to the casino."

Mrs. Anderson didn't look like she appreciated anything about any part of this deal, but she began to jot some numbers down on a sheet of paper.

"There are several ways we can set this up for you." She was peering over her glasses at Mildred. "It just depends how you would like to receive the funds."

"How do you mean?" Mildred was suppressing an urge to dance around the office.

"It can be set up as monthly, yearly, or lump sum. I recommend monthly, of course."

Mildred was quiet for a moment then said, "I think I'd like the lump sum." That would sever her connection to the casino immediately, no checks coming in monthly or yearly.

"Really? It won't be earning any interest."

"I see that...it's just that I might be able to use it to buy a small condominium. I have a cousin in Phoenix who has been after me to move there. I'd have to get a job of course. I'd want to get a job, actually."

"But you don't want to continue working here?" Mrs. Anderson was becoming more skeptical by the minute and Mildred hoped she wasn't causing the offer to be retracted, but Mr. Black stepped in once more and smoothed things over.

"I can see how Miss Alcott would like to change her surroundings, Mrs. Anderson. The gentleman who's missing was her boss for all of the time that she worked here," he looked at Mildred. "Isn't that right?"

"Yes, it is. He never missed a day in all of those years...so it's very sad to come in each day and see his empty desk."

"There, you see Mrs. Anderson? The working environment is just not right for Miss Alcott anymore."

Mrs. Anderson just raised her eyebrows and resumed the note taking.

Mildred looked around the empty apartment. A small moving company had packed up everything and moved it into her storage unit. She had ridden her bike behind the truck, made sure that everything was stored, and then padlocked the unit. When she got back to her apartment she leaned the bike up against the building and felt sure that it would be gone by morning. She wiped down the kitchen counters once more, picked up her suitcase, went into the hallway and closed the door behind her.

She knocked on the door of the manager's apartment and glanced at her watch. The taxi should be here soon.

"Oh, Miss Alcott. Are you leaving now?'

"Yes, Mrs. Crowley, I'm off."

"Well, we're going to miss you. You've been a good tenant all these years. Real quiet." She took the keys that Mildred handed her. "Do you want to leave me a forwarding address? In case you get some mail?"

"I don't have an address yet, Mrs. Crowley. I've put a hold on any mail at the post office and when I can I'll send them a change of address... when I know where I'll be." Mildred hadn't received any mail, other than grocery store coupons and political ads, at this address in years. Any mail of importance went to her post office box under the name of O'Malley. She had redirected that mail to the villa in France, and then closed the box.

"Well, good-by then Miss Alcott. And good luck to you."

It *was* good-by to Miss Alcott ...and hello to Miss O'Malley, and her luck seemed to be holding.

April 2014

Chapter 27

Grimaud, France
Villa Tournesol

Mildred stood at the edge of the terrace looking out over the trees and the tops of the red tiled roofs in the village lower down on the hillside, and on to the sea glimmering in the distance in the fading afternoon sun.

"Madam, I thought you might enjoy an aperitif before dinner." Berenice appeared carrying a tray with a glass, a split of champagne, and a small plate of hors d'oeuvres.

"Thank you Berenice. It's just the thing I need."

"Shall I open the bottle for you, Madame?"

"Please. I'm not good with those corks." She didn't mention that this was her first glass of champagne.

"I hope you are pleased with the house." Berenice set the tray on a table close to the pool and began opening the bottle.

They had finished the tour of the villa and the agency had seen to it that each room was provided with fresh flowers, the linen closet was full, and the kitchen was stocked with food and drink for at least a week.

"Berenice, I couldn't be happier. Everything is perfect. I feel like I've come home...after a very long trip."

"Oui, Madame. It is a very comfortable home." She tied a small napkin around the neck of the champagne bottle and set it on the tray. "There is a small salad for your dinner in the refrigerator, and a plate of fruit and cheese on the counter, but I could prepare something warm, if you like."

"Oh no, the salad is fine. You go on home...you've done enough for today. Will you be back tomorrow? "

"Oui, certainement. I can be here as often as you like."

"Then every day...not weekends, of course." Mildred knew she would be glad of the companionship. Berenice was the only person in Grimaud that she knew at this point. "You can start helping me with my French."

"Oh yes, we'll start right away. Perhaps tomorrow we can explore the village. The shops and markets are a good place to begin learning a language, especially the markets." She laughed. "Somehow I think the words for food are the easiest to learn."

"I think you're right. We'll start with food."

Berenice hesitated, and then said, "Do you have friends in Grimaud?"

"No one, Berenice, just you."

"Then I will introduce you to many nice people tomorrow, French *and* American, if you like."

"Oui, certainement," She smiled at Berenice. "How was that?"

"Très bien Madame. And now I wish you a good evening, bonsoir, and I will be here in the morning. Nine o'clock?"

"Yes, that's fine. Bonsoir...and merci...for everything."

Mildred could hear the front door click shut as she poured a glass of champagne. She returned to the edge of the terrace and watched the lights winking on in the village and the stars beginning to brighten in the evening sky. She was filled with so many conflicting feelings that she couldn't be sure if she was thrilled or terrified. So many things had fallen into place over the years that this seemed inevitable, that she was a landed property owner in Ireland *and* France. Something could go wrong, of course, but there was no point worrying about that now. There had always been a solution to the many roadblocks over the years, but she was still puzzled by Mr. Black, and she knew Mrs. Anderson was too. He obviously wanted her to leave the casino, but why? Maybe there was someone else coming from Atlantic City with the new boss and they were getting her job, or maybe he was in cahoots with Mr. Cravetz and they wanted her out of the way. She did know too much. Maybe he just felt sorry for her. Whatever the reason, she was glad to accept the offer.

She often wondered what happened to Mr. Cravetz. If she had been in his place, she knew what she would have done – use the vacation week to disappear with the gold. She would have parked the car in the airport parking lot, bought a ticket under an assumed name, and vanished. But that was only plausible if you knew he had the gold, so it was never a theory explored by the police. She knew it would be a blow to him when he discovered that probably more than half of the kilo bars were fakes, but she didn't feel bad about that. He still had an enormous sum of money to retire on...and so did she.

"Mr. Cravetz...George...I feel like I can call you that," she lifted her glass toward the sea, "Here's to you. I hope you're happy, wherever you are."

She finished the champagne in her glass and carried the tray back to the kitchen. She could see that she wasn't going to get the cork back into the bottle so she just poured the rest into her glass and sat down at the dining room table with her salad and her view of the sea.

September 2014

Chapter 28

Kansas City

The oppressive summer heat and the lack of any breeze left the gauzy curtains hanging limp beside the open window. Birds sang earlier in the day but had now taken cover from the approaching storm. The darkening skies had turned a gray-green and a blinding flash of light accompanied by an almost simultaneous clap of thunder announced its arrival. Addie crossed the room to the open window and could feel the cool wind that presaged the coming downpour. She let the breeze blow through her hair to cool her off and then pulled the sash down as the rain began to fall.

Michael followed her into the room, switched on the overhead light, and laid a few tools down on the dresser. "Well, we almost made it. This is the last room to pack up."

"Typical moving day. I guess it wouldn't be complete without rain." She looked around at the furniture in Mr. Barker's old room. "Maybe the storm will pass by the time we get this bed apart. It looks like a project with a capital P."

"How old do you think it is?"

"Rose said it probably came out from the east with their grandmother when she came here as a young bride, so at least a hundred years, maybe more. Which makes it a genuine antique."

"And it makes your aunts very generous to give it to us. I'm sure Rose could get a good price for it at the store."

In the three months that Addie and Michael had been married they discovered themselves the beneficiary of many family heirlooms: a set of china for twelve, and the silverware to go with it; a silver tea and coffee service; silver platters; and table linens by the drawer full. Addie was grateful for all of it because they were family treasures, but could hardly imagine the time when she would use it. Michael's house, and Addie's now, was a different style altogether. Hand thrown pottery and rustic pieces were more apropos. Maybe when the holidays rolled around she would break out the silver polish and set a table that Helen and Rose would enjoy.

Another thing that Addie discovered is how quickly the tempo of life can change. A year ago her future, when she thought about her future, was lost in a mist. She had her aunts to think about, and the store, but beyond that things were fuzzy. Now she had Michael and a future that they could both visualize, and did, for hours on end. They talked of children, and his business, and travel, and the coming winter with warm fires, and the possibility of adding a second story to the house with a screened in sleeping porch to ward off the no-see-ums, an actual category of pesky insect. And they laughed about the gold bars squirreled away inside the walls and the men captured in the basement. Once Michael asked her if she was sorry that they hadn't kept at least one of the kilo bars and Addie thought about it. But in the end, it seemed the right thing to do, returning all of it.

They were doing ok now. Michael brought his furniture to the shop and they began to build up some interest in his work. Addie took over his jewelry and accessory business, which he was glad to relinquish, so that he could concentrate on his woodworking. She still had time for the store, and her aunts, so all in all everything was working out just fine.

"Let's get the mattress off of the bed and see if it comes apart in sections." Michael was examining the joints and posts of the bed.

"Don't all beds come apart in sections?" Addie teased.

"Ha! They do." Michael smiled and tapped the top part of the post at one corner of the bed. "This is what I hope will come off.

These bedposts must be seven feet tall. It sure will be easier to move the bed frame if they're off."

Addie began stripping the bedding and bundled it up to take to the basement. "One last load for 'this old house,'" she laughed. "We might as well pack the sheets clean." She helped him hoist the mattress and the old wire springs off of the bed and lean them up against the wall. Then she gathered up the sheets and coverlet and headed for the basement.

"Hurry back. I know I'll need your help when I start taking this thing apart."

Addie passed Rose in the dining room wrapping some figurines in packing paper and neatly stowing them in a small moving box. The moving van was coming in the morning.

"This is the last of the lot." Rose gestured toward the china cabinet. "Everything else can go to the store for sale."

Addie and Michael were both taken by surprise when they returned from their honeymoon to hear from Rose and Helen that they had decided to sell the house. They said it was too big for just the two of them and they really weren't interested in trying to rent out Mr. Barker's room. Helen said she just wouldn't feel right about someone else in that room after all those years with Mr. Barker. Addie was relieved because she had thought it might not be the wisest idea, getting someone you didn't know to move in with two elderly women, no matter what kind of references they gave. So the house had gone on the market at a reasonable price, and a young family, with three children, was moving in next week. Helen and Rose had found a sweet little Victorian house in a small town close to Addie and Michael. Not too close, just close enough. Addie would be able to pick Rose up each morning to ride into the store while Helen remained happily at home, cleaning, cooking, and just generally looking out for the two of them. Things were good.

Addie hurried up from the basement where she left Helen managing the laundry. When she came back into the bedroom,

Michael was peering closely at the section of the bedpost where the spindle joined the post.

"There's a line here that looks like this top part of the post might unscrew, or come off somehow." He was gently moving the top part of the post back and forth. "They usually made these old four posters in sections so that they could be broken down for shipping...there was less risk of breaking the posts." Soon his efforts were rewarded with a scraping sound and then, as he twisted it, the spindle began to lift out of the post. "Great, it's coming apart...just like a cork out of a bottle. This will sure make it easier to move." He lifted the post out and laid it down by the wall.

As he began working on the next post, Addie peered into the hole left by the one he had removed. "How did they make this hole? It's amazing that the pieces fit together so exactly."

"They would have used a router. But it was all handwork, no power tools in those days. They were amazing craftsmen."

Addie looked up at Michael. "There's something in the bottom of the hole...and it's probably not insulation."

Michael gave her a quizzical look. "What do you mean?"

"Take a look."

"Well for god's sake!" He shook his head. "I don't believe it."

"It's gold, right?"

"Yes. It looks like a coin." He tried to fish it out but he needed something thin to slip down the side to pry it up. "Do you have a nail file, or something like it?"

"Maybe. Let me look in the bathroom. I haven't packed it up yet." Addie hurried down the hall, rummaged through several drawers in the dressing table next to the sink and came up with a metal file.

"Here, try this," she said handing it to Michael.

He slipped the file between the inside of the bedpost and the coin and flipped it up on edge. "My fingers are too big, you'll have to get it."

Addie retrieved the coin and then said to Michael, "There's more."

"Of course there is. Mr. Barker was no slouch when it came to gold."

They proceeded to fish four more coins out of the bedpost.

"It says 'fifty dollars,'" Addie said as she examined the coins more closely. "What're all these worth? Two hundred and fifty dollars?"

"More. It also says 'one ounce fine gold'...which would make each one worth whatever the market price is. It was twelve hundred dollars an ounce last year."

"So even at that price...where's your calculator?"

"I can do this one in my head...six thousand dollars." He stared at Addie. "I guess I better start taking these other posts apart."

They ended up with the bedposts disassembled and twenty coins stacked on the dresser.

Michael showed Addie the raw end of one of the spindles. "You can see that he just sawed off about an inch and a half from the end of each of these, which was enough to allow the coins to fit inside and the spindle to sit snuggly back down on the post. Very clever."

"Michael, these coins weren't even mentioned last year when our friends from Las Vegas were leaving. They said they thought there could be nine more kilo bars. They must not have known about missing coins or they would have mentioned them, don't you think?"

"You know those kilo bars really could be here. I never thought to look further than the paneling for them." Michael looked around the room. "Maybe we should start taking the woodwork apart."

"It's sad, really, when you think about it," Addie ran her hand over the footboard of the bed, which was still standing. "It seems like Mr. Barker spent his entire life on this project. Years of plotting and building and probably looking over his shoulder all of the time. And then he drops dead. I wonder what he planned to do with all of his treasure?"

"Well, it looked like he was planning on taking two hundred and eighty bars, but that meant at least another year. Maybe he started cashing them in and that's where the nine bars went."

"That makes sense. However, if he followed his usual modus operandi then he probably hid the cash under the wallpaper. Maybe we should strip the walls," she laughed.

"You're on," he grinned, "right after we get this bed apart."

Michael was inspecting the joint where the side rail attached to the bedpost. "Here's where it screws together," and he rotated a decorative brass medallion that was on the outside of the leg. Underneath, sunk in a hole was the head of the large screw that held the bed together. "Before I take this screw out I need to get the slats off, and then we need something to support the sides when the footboard comes off. I don't want to split the wood at the other end."

While Addie looked for something to support the sides, Michael began to remove the screws from the bed slats. There were twelve slats spaced out and screwed to the ledger attached to the rail. As he worked his way from the foot of the bed to the head, he found that the screw in the last slat, by the headboard was different. By this time Addie had come back with two small packing boxes to support the sides.

"Look at this, " he said showing her two of the screws that he had removed. "Eleven of the screws are like this one and are very old, probably made before 1850."

"How do you know that?"

"Before that time screws were all handmade and so the slot on the top wasn't always in the center, like these." He pointed to the small pile on the dresser. "But not only is the slot in the middle of the screw head on this last one, it's shiny. It's new." He headed around the bed. "Let me take the screw out on the other side."

Addie had bent down to inspect the slats and she pointed out that that last one was slightly taller than the rest. "Do you think it had to be replaced? It's not the same size as the others."

"Maybe." He was drawing the screw out of the hole. He lifted the slat up off of the bed. "Boy this thing is heavy." He stared at it for a moment, turning it back and forth and then whistled. "Oh brother, I bet we found the nine missing bars."

"We did?"

Michael laid the slat, upside down, on the other slats. "The bottom of this is a new piece of wood." There was a small screw head at each end of the slat. He quickly removed them and gently lifted the bottom away. There, in a neat row, lay nine small tissue-wrapped packages, end to end, with additional tissue wadded up between them.

Addie sucked in her breath. "I can't believe it." She looked up at Michael. "Why would he do this and not put these bars in the wall?"

"I'm just guessing, but this may have been his original hiding place before he came up with the wall paneling idea. But even if he put all of these bars in here at the same time, it meant hoisting the mattress and springs off by himself, altering the slat, and putting the bed back together. He couldn't hope to keep doing that without Helen noticing all of that commotion at some point."

"So he created his honeycomb all around the walls."

"He could explain the building project as an improvement to the room and never cause any suspicion." Michael looked at the piece of wood, still in his hands, that he had removed from the slat. "This is really very simple to build. It's just a long skinny box top, a piece of plywood with narrow strips of wood... glued it looks like...around the edges. It's deep enough to hold the kilo bars and that's all. He had to use new screws though to attach the slat back to the bed because the old ones wouldn't have been long enough with this added wood. But it was too cumbersome to keep hiding it this way." He leaned the wooden box top against the wall. "Besides, he could only hide a hundred and thirty-five bars in the bed and it looks like he had bigger plans."

"So what do we do now?" She was looking at the gold still lying on the slat.

"Well, we need someplace to put this that's secure, it's a lot of money to just have laying around...then finish this move. I don't know. What are you thinking?"

"I guess we better give that Charles Black a call. I probably still have that number he gave us." She paused for a minute. "You know, I was thinking that maybe it was alright to not make a call about the coins...since they were never mentioned. But these bars are too much, ... don't you think?"

They were tossing the 'thinking' ball back and forth and there was an obvious innuendo attached to the thoughts. What if they didn't call?

After a minute Michael nodded. "It's too much alright. We *should* call. But first we need to get this bed loaded in the truck. It's stopped raining but it could start again anytime. Can you find something to put all of this gold in for the time being? Maybe a shoebox?" They had begun stacking the bars on the dresser next to the coins.

Addie unwrapped one and shook her head. "Hard to believe something this small can be worth so much. What do you think? Forty or fifty thousand?" She handed the bar to Michael.

"I don't know what the market price is these days, but that's what it was worth last year. Closer to fifty."

"Let me go find something to put all of this in." While Michael went back to unscrewing the rest of the slats, Addie again went down the hall to the bathroom. It was the only room upstairs not completely packed. There were no boxes of any kind so she emptied out her old make-up bag.

"They look like candy bars," she said as she loaded the gold bars and coins into the pouch and zipped it shut.

By this time Michael had removed all of the slats and Addie held on to the footboard while he took the screws out of the side rails. Together they carried all of the sections of the bed down the stairs and loaded them into their truck. The headboard was the last piece to go. As they lifted it away from the wall they could see a bag of some sort hanging from a small hook on the back of the bed.

"Uh oh. More surprises," Michael said.

It was hanging closer to Addie's side and she reached for it. "What now?" The bag was one of the sort that travelers wear under their shirts to protect their money or passport. "There's something in it. Maybe another bar...I wouldn't be surprised if we started finding them in the light fixtures. Wait...not a bar." She had opened the bag and pulled out a wallet. "Oh look." She flipped it open. "It's his other ID." She handed the wallet to Michael. "It belongs to his alter ego...George Cravetz. When he died the only ID we found was for Samuel Barker. With our address, no less."

"He must have switched it when he came into town. The back of this bed made a good hiding place. Nobody could move this without help, certainly not you girls...sorry, ladies." Addie's raised eyebrows caused him to amend his statement. "You know what I mean. Anyway, he could just reach behind the bed and get the bag. He really thought of everything, didn't he?"

"It seems like it's all he thought about. Like I said...sad."

After wrestling with the bed, taping up packing boxes, folding the laundry, and the final push to make sure the house was ready for the new owners, they were all exhausted.

"I'm ready to go home." Rose was winding the electrical cord around the base of a very pretty lamp. "I'll take this with me in the car. It's too hard to pack." She set it on the dining room table and began putting other odds and ends into a shopping bag. Addie had set the make-up bag on the table when she came downstairs and now Rose picked it up. "Good heavens! What's in here? I'd think it was the kitchen sink if the bag was bigger!"

Addie grinned and shook her head. "Rose, Helen...Michael and I have a little story to tell you. It seems we're not quite finished with the Mr. Barker saga."

"Whatever are you talking about?" Rose was looking at the heavy bag in her hands. "Is it about this?"

"Yes, it is. You'd better sit down."

Chapter 29

"Did my aunts shock you?" Addie was clutching the bag of gold in her lap as Michael turned off the highway onto the road that led to their house.

"Well...yes, as a matter of fact, they did." He laughed. "Not really. It was more of a surprise than a shock."

When Rose and Helen learned about the new find, they were against the idea of giving it back.

"I don't see any point to it now," Rose said. "We sent all of that other gold back with those men so they wouldn't lose their jobs. We've never heard anything from them, not even a thank you, so I say we keep it."

"Oh I agree with Rose. I'm sure we should keep it. Mr. Barker would have wanted us to have it." Helen's eyes looked a little misty, as usual when the subject of Mr. Barker came up. "After all of the time he spent carrying it away from that place...just to see it all go back. I don't think we should do that to him."

But finally they all agreed that Michael should give the man, Charles Black, a call. He wouldn't mention the coins though, unless it came up.

Michael pulled the car up to the house and they got out. It was late but the summer sun, just setting, spread a warm glow over the landscape.

"How about a bite to eat out here on the veranda?" Addie asked.

"That's a good idea. I'll tell you what, you go stash that bag someplace and see if you can find that phone number." Michael held the door open for her and then headed for the kitchen. "I'll see what I can find to eat and I'll meet you outside." He glanced at his watch. "We can give that guy a call. It's early in Las Vegas."

Addie had to rummage around in the papers and files that she had brought with her when she moved into this house, but it was there, on the back of a hotel parking lot receipt. When she came back to the porch, Michael was just opening up a bottle of wine. He'd set out bread, cheese, olives, and salami."

"Oh, this looks so good." Addie realize how hungry she was.

"What do you think? Candles?"

"Absolutely! I'll get them."

They sat, relaxed, close to each other, picking at the crumbs that were left and just breathing in the warm summer evening and listening to the song of the tree frogs. After the rain, the land smelled fresh and everything was good.

"I hate to break the mood, but why don't I make that call." He reached into his pocket for his cell phone.

"Yes, do. I'm feeling magnanimous at the moment. Better call before the feeling goes away."

He punched in the numbers on the paper and listened. "It's ringing."

"Hello." It was a woman's voice.

"I'm trying to reach Charles Black."

"Well, you have the right number but it doesn't belong to him anymore. It's been mine for the last six months, but I'm still getting calls for him."

"Oh, I'm sorry." Michael gave Addie a puzzled look. "So, you don't know where I can reach him?"

"No, I don't! I have no idea who he is. He must not have given a new number to *anyone*. I know it's not your fault, but this is getting really annoying1"

"I'm sorry," Michael repeated himself. "Thanks anyway, and I won't call this number again."

"Good!" The line went dead.

They looked at each other for a minute. "So...do you remember the name of the casino where they worked?" Michael refilled their glasses.

"Not right off the top of my head. It's probably in my computer history." She didn't make a move to go look.

"It's not a good idea to just have that stuff sitting around the house. Maybe we should look into a safety deposit box." He swirled the wine around in his glass, breathed in the bouquet, and took a sip.

"What about getting a safe?" Addie ate the last olive in the bowl.

"The problem with that is now people *think* you might have something worth stealing."

"That's a good point."

They were quiet for a while, just sipping their wine and gazing into the night. The fireflies had appeared and were dancing across the lawn.

"Here's a crazy idea," Addie said at last. "What if we just sleep on it?"

"You mean talk about it tomorrow?"

"No. I really mean sleep on it...what if... when we put the bed back together...we put the gold back where Mr. Barker had it. It will be there if those gentlemen from Las Vegas ever ask...and if they don't..."

Michael gave her a long look. "You know...that's a brilliant idea, but are you sure you're going to be ok with it? I mean, you've said before that it was the 'right thing to do' to give it back."

"Yes, I know." Addie looked out into the darkness spread before her. "I don't really want the money. I don't think we need it...we're doing fine. But...it does give a certain sense of security, don't you think?" She stopped, and then smiled. "I'm not sure we have to rush to give it back. I think my aunts would agree."

"And so would Mr. Barker."

"Yes he would. It's like Aunt Helen said, he worked hard to carry all of that gold away. It's too bad to waste all of his efforts."

"Indeed." Michael refilled their glasses. "I think we should drink a toast to Mr. Barker."

"Good idea. What should it be?"

"How about ... 'Here's to Samuel Barker, our accidental benefactor.'"

"That's good."

The clink of their glasses floated on the breeze.

The End

"All that glisters is not gold…"
William Shakespeare, *The Merchant of Venice*

Made in the USA
Columbia, SC
21 June 2017